# Magenta McPhee

### Catherine Bateson

Holiday House / New York

First published by Woolshed Press in Australia 2009
Woolshed Press is a trademark of Random House Australia Pty Ltd.
100 Pacific Highway, North Sydney, Australia, NSW 2060
The moral right of the author has been asserted.
First published in the United States of America by Holiday House in 2010
HOLIDAY HOUSE is registered in the U.S. Patent and Trademark Office.
Printed and Bound in December 2009 at Maple Vail, Binghamton, NY, USA.
www.holidayhouse.com
First American Edition
1   3   5   7   9   10   8   6   4   2

Library of Congress Cataloging-in-Publication Data

Bateson, Catherine, 1960–
Magenta McPhee / Catherine Bateson. — 1st American ed.
p. cm.
Summary: Thinking her father needs a new interest in his life after he is laid-off of
work, teenaged Magenta, who envisions herself as a future fantasy author, decides to
dabble in matchmaking which brings unexpected results.
ISBN 978-0-8234-2253-1 (hardcover)
[1. Fathers and daughters—Fiction.   2. Authorship—Fiction.   3. Dating (Social
customs)—Fiction.   4. Single parent families—Fiction.   5. Australia—Fiction.]
I. Title.
PZ7.B3222Mag 2010
[Fic]—dc22
2009010854

# Contents

# First Publication

Not only was the letter—my letter—printed, but it was also the Fave of the Month. I won a Sammi Girl T-shirt (pink with a red heart), a bottle of fake tanner, a CD from some try-hard girlie singer and a 1 GB MP3 player (again pink with a red heart) that tried as hard as the girlie singer to look like a real brand name. I didn't care. I was a published writer.

My letter read:

Dear Dr. Suzie,

My name is Magenta, and my parents split up quite a while ago, but while my mother has moved on and is remarrying in a few months, my father, Max, has slumped into a depression bigger than a humpback whale. He's lost his job—due to a downturn in his industry—and he seems to spend a lot of time reading too many books at the local library. He's also on an anti-technology crusade, which I don't think is helping his chances of getting a job, as he's in IT. My mother insists it's up to him to help himself, but I can't help feeling he needs a helping hand. I love him, and I'm worried. I've tried bullying, gentle persuasion, and emotional blackmail. I've now threatened not to clean my room until he gets a life. He doesn't care. He wades through the mess on the floor and refuses to comment. I refuse to go the next step—sacrifice my grades and take up with bad boys or heavy metal. But I am desperate. Any ideas?

Magenta-Mad-at-Dad

And Dr. Suzie's reply appeared beneath it:

Dear Magenta,

Your mom's right. Your dad's mental health is not your responsibility! He's the adult. It sounds as though he's going through a rough patch at the moment, but perhaps all he needs is a little time. If you want to point out to him that you think he is depressed, you could tell him about organizations like Blue Day or suggest he talk to someone. He might be going through a period of readjustment. Losing a job isn't easy for anyone. Going to the local library is a positive sign. So don't worry too much. Just remember, it must make him feel a lot better knowing he has the support of such a loyal daughter. Keep getting those grades!

Dr. Suzie

P.S. Have you thought about being a writer? You've got a great turn of phrase there!

Really, the best part of the whole letter was the P.S. I read it over and over at breakfast until Dad told me to put that silly magazine away and concentrate on my muesli. As if muesli ever needed anyone's undivided attention. I longed to show him—but I could hardly let him read just the P.S., and the rest of the letter was private and about him. I wanted to call my mom, but I couldn't tell her, either. She might get all guilt-stricken and cancel the wedding or something. So I rolled the magazine and stuck it in my bag for school. I'd show Polly, my bestest friend in the whole world. She refused to read *Sammi* because she'd once counted the advertisements in it. But she'd read the letter. After all, she'd helped write it.

"You off?" Dad asked from the bedroom door, keeping his gaze strictly at eye level.

"Almost," I said. "Dad, have you heard of Blue Day?"

Dad grunted, "If it's that band day in the park, no, Magenta, you're far too young."

"I think that's Big Day Out," I said. "This is different."

"That's a relief. I didn't think you were into all that, Mags."

"Please don't call me Mags," I said automatically, "and no, Dad, you have to be a teenager for that kind of thing. I'm not developmentally up to that yet."

"It's hard to tell," Dad said gloomily, looking me up and down. "One day you're gurgling in a stroller, and the next you're wearing fake tattoos and reading magazines that don't even have proper names. Also, can you please tell me when this silly moratorium on cleaning is going to stop? I hate having to keep my eyes on the ceiling every time I come in, and it's an occupational health-and-safety issue. You could actually kill me doing this, you know. I walk in, eyes on the ceiling, trip on some kind of discarded footwear, or my foot gets stuck in a pair of tights. I fall, hit my head on the corner of the bed, and that's it. I bleed to death while you're at school. You come home and find me dead. But that's not the worst of it. I've ruined the science project you've spent four weeks of your life doing."

"What are you doing in my room when I'm not here?" I ignored him. Dad enjoyed worst-case scenarios.

"The normal things. Trying to collect laundry, finding the notes the school sends home with you, dusting the light fixtures . . ."

"Snooping."

"Parental management."

I was glad I took my journal to school every day, even though that put it at risk to be snatched by the boys. At least I could keep my eye on *them*.

"I don't need managing," I pointed out. "I manage myself quite well, thank you."

"We all need managing, pet," Dad said, scuffing some socks over to a pile of other socks. "I'm assuming these are all dirty?"

"Probably." I shrugged. "It would be easier on both of us if you admitted that *you* needed some management at this point. Then I could clean my room."

I could tell by the tightening of Dad's mouth that I'd gone too far. If I wasn't careful, I'd get a "young lady" right about now.

"Young lady"—See? I knew it!—"I've told you, I'm reassessing. There have been a lot of changes, and I'm working out what I want to do for the rest of my life. It's adult stuff, Mags—adult. Obviously I can't make you understand that, but I'm asking you, yet again, to accept what I'm saying and end this stupid campaign."

I stuck my chin out and lifted my head. It's a well-known fact that most people who are really depressed can't admit it. It was in our health class. And we were told to keep an eye on anyone we thought might be suffering. EAR—Eyes Ask Reach. I'd been reaching for weeks, but Dad was avoiding me.

"I'll think about my room this weekend," I said. "Think—not necessarily do anything." I was getting a bit sick of it, too. Dad was right, when I thought about it. It was an occupational health-and-safety issue. I didn't believe for one second that Dad would die on my science project, but even a dirty footprint could ruin all the work I'd done.

"You'll do more than think about it," Dad warned, but I was nearly out the door by then, so I could pretend I hadn't heard him.

Polly was late, so I had to wait until recess to show her my first published piece of writing.

"See?" she said when we'd both read it three times over. "I told you; you're going to be a writer, Magenta. This is the first positive evidence, but it won't be the last. You're on your way to fame and fortune."

Polly likes making big statements. I wasn't so sure about the fortune bit. The last time we'd had a visiting writer at school, he'd looked a little frayed around the edges, I thought. Someone had asked him if he'd ever met J.K. Rowling, and that really set him off. He was still ranting when the bell rang and most people were out the door. I'd felt sorry for him. I knew what he meant. Just thinking about Harry Potter gave me writer's block, too.

"It's just a letter," I said, "and I'd have to say, Polly, that it's not particularly helpful. But I do like the P.S."

"I think we're going to have to take your dad in hand ourselves," Polly said. "Clearly we're the only ones who know he's in trouble. I suggest a meeting at my place on the weekend. I'll talk to Jane about it in a roundabout way and do some research on the Internet. Do you think your dad will let you sleep over?"

"After I clean my room he will, but that could take all weekend."

"Nonsense," Polly said firmly. "Tell you what, I'll drop over first thing Saturday and help you clean. It's above and beyond, of course—but I'll do it for you."

Dad welcomed the idea of Polly coming to help me clean.

"She's got a real practical bent, that girl," he said, "for all her eccentricities."

"You should talk," I said rather sharply. "You've become just as bad!"

"I have chosen to downsize my technological dependencies, but that is hardly eccentric. It's just common sense."

"It's ridiculous not even having a cell phone, Dad. What if there's an emergency?"

"There are very few emergencies that have relied on a cell phone. Anyway, you've got one, so what's the big deal?"

"That's the big deal—you use mine. It's just hypocritical."

"I don't use yours. Your mother occasionally calls me on your cell phone on matters she considers can't possibly wait until we're back home from wherever we've been. She's always been impatient."

"At least she lives in this century," I muttered, but Dad pretended not to hear me.

Since he'd been laid off, Dad had gotten rid of most of our gadgets, as he called them. We no longer had a dishwasher, a clothes dryer, or a microwave. He'd kept the freezer, because it allowed us to buy seasonally and freeze. I made him keep the TV and the DVD player, although he hadn't wanted to. He voluntarily kept his computer, so he could look for a new job. He sold his cell phone, his laptop, and his PDA on eBay and went out and bought a diary and an address book instead. He bought a pasta machine but gave the bread maker to my mother. The pasta machine, he pointed out, didn't require electricity. We've made pasta once.

I thought he'd gone a bit bonkers. It was part of the depression. He could call it downsizing or whatever he liked, but it was clearly the behavior of someone suffering from some kind of emotional and mental problem.

It's different from Polly not using electricity except when strictly necessary. That's a phase she's going through, or so Jane, her mom, says. She's Green—well, apart from her computer use, which I'd say pushes her into the red zone. But there is something quite beautiful about walking into her candlelit bedroom. You could actually blame Jane. She started Green Box Caterers just before anyone else thought about organic veggies or recycled cardboard plates. She's now a caterer to the stars. She specializes in photo shoots. It's no wonder Polly is eccentric, given that her dad is a pessimistic sculptor and her mom an upbeat cook.

"The last time Polly helped me clean up," I told Dad, "she threw away most of my stuff, and I had to spend the next day rescuing it."

"One day that girl will have a de-cluttering business," Dad said, "and make a fortune, if she inherits her mom's business sense."

I checked him out quickly. I think other people earning money must get him down when he's unemployed. But he sounded cheerful enough. Of course, you can't tell. Depressed people get good at hiding their true feelings behind lighthearted jokes. I'd read that somewhere.

Polly arrived at ten on Saturday morning.

"What are you wearing?" I asked when I opened the door to her. She had a bandanna wrapped around her head, rubber boots on her feet, and latex gloves on her hands.

"Cleaning clothes, of course. Where are yours?"

"My room's not a toxic-waste dump," I said, eyeing the gloves.

"Oh, isn't it?" Dad interrupted. "Hi, Polly, how are things?"

"With me—fine. But life as we know it is doomed." Polly

spoke with gloomy pleasure. "People of your generation, Max, are responsible, and my generation was probably born too late to reverse the damage."

"Well, well," Dad said. "Nothing like an optimistic view to brighten up your Saturday morning."

"I'm not a pessimist," Polly said, "just realistic. If I was pessimistic, I wouldn't bother trying to do anything about it."

"We all have to do our bit," Dad said. "Tea, coffee?"

"I don't drink anything with caffeine," Polly said, "and anyway, coffee exploits third-world countries."

"Water? Milk?"

"No, thanks, Max. Really, I'm fine."

"I'll leave you girls to it, then. I'm going to the library. Any overdue books, Magenta?"

I shook my head. I couldn't afford to take out library books anymore. I still had a fine on my card that I hadn't paid.

"The only place he goes these days is the library," I told Polly as she surveyed my room. "He used to play golf and do other stuff, but now it's always the library."

"Golf's expensive," Polly said, "and boring."

"Dad says he only played it for business, but I think he's lying. He had his own set of golf clubs. He sold them. Sometimes I think he's sold his life."

"Well, we'll clean this up. It's not quite as bad as I thought it might be, although whatever was in that lunch box has become a health hazard."

"Oh, that." I looked at it with interest. "I think that might have been dip once."

"It's disgusting." Polly pulled her bandanna down over her nose and carried the lunch box into the kitchen.

"You can borrow my gloves to wash it."

"Can't we just chuck it?"

"Magenta! We're Green, remember? It's a perfectly good lunch box underneath that mold." She peeled off her gloves, and I put them on reluctantly.

Finally my room was neat enough. I drew the line at Polly organizing my books into alphabetical order or tidying any drawers that could just be closed on the mess inside.

"Okay," she said, propping Teddy up against the pillows so he looked uncomfortably straight, rather than his usual slumped self, "now we work on your other problem. Get a piece of paper, Magenta. We're going to do this scientifically."

By the time Dad came home from the library, we had googled "depression" and written our list.

| | |
|---|---|
| *Problem:* | Depression |
| *Signs:* | Being alone, not going out, not getting a job, getting rid of stuff, not having a girlfriend |
| *Cause:* | The Divorce, The Layoff |
| *Solution:* | Get interested in life again |
| *How?* | |

"Well, you have a good time, girls," Dad said as he dropped us off at Polly's house.

"Are you sure you'll be okay?" I asked for the third time. I felt bad leaving him all alone on a weekend after we'd written about his problem. He'd probably be twice as depressed—all alone on a Saturday night.

"What's all this sudden concern?" Dad said, and dropped a kiss on the top of my head. "Think I can't order Chinese takeout without you?"

"See?" Polly hissed as he drove away. "Reliance on fast food. Jane says interest in food wanes with depression—either that or binge eating starts."

"Dad likes takeout," I said. "We had Chinese food on Saturdays even when Mom and Dad were still married."

"Well, there you are: he's not moving on, is he? I bet your mom doesn't still have them."

"No, we go out for Thai, because Trib loves it."

"See? Your mom's moved on—Thai and Trib. What more evidence do you need?"

"Chinese food tells us nothing about my Dad." Sometimes I have to fight hard against Polly's mania for evidence. She can get things wrong, but it's hard to remember that because she's so smart most of the time.

"Whatever. It's part of a pattern. Patterns are important. I'm exploring patterns at the moment. I'm . . . but this is a dark secret, Magenta. You mustn't tell anyone."

"You've got a secret you haven't told me?"

"It's very recent. I only started doing it last night, and I could hardly call you at ten o'clock, could I?"

We sat down on Polly's bed. She had a purple comforter with silver stars scattered over it. There were no teddies or stuffed toys. They were just traps for dust mites, Jane said. A large bookcase on one wall had books in it two-deep. They were all arranged, first by category and then in alphabetical order by author's last name. She had a big, L-shaped desk with a computer, printer, and scanner on it and nothing else except for a dozen tea-light candles. Nothing had changed.

"What's the secret, then?"

"I think I'm a witch!" she said, paused, and then looked at me, her brown eyes so wide I could see the whites all around them.

"A witch?"

She nodded. "I don't see why patterns in words can't be as important as patterns in numbers. And patterns in numbers make things happen. Take your times tables, for example. All that is really is a pattern of numbers, right?"

"I guess . . ."

"Well, it's the same with words. If you start repeating words in spells, then the pattern itself might be enough to make it happen. If you have the right kind of brain."

"The right kind of brain?" I knew I wasn't sounding particularly smart, but this whole conversation was bizarre.

"I may have the right kind of brain," Polly said, smoothing the quilt under her fingers. "Last night I put together my first spell—a simple pattern of words, repeating one main word in different combinations. Want to hear it?"

"I guess . . ."

"Okay, but I'm going to say it normally rather than as a spell, because it's worked once, and that's enough."

"Okay . . ."

"Jinx Jeremy, Jeremy Jinx. Bitter is the taste he drinks. Jinx Jeremy, Jeremy Jinx. Drinks he bitter inks. Inks Jeremy Jinx. Bitter is the taste he inks. Jinx Jeremy, Jeremy Jinx."

"Right." It sounded good, even when said normally. I didn't know what it meant, except that Jeremy was Polly's little brother and sometimes he got to be too much for her, so I assumed the spell was against him in some way.

"So, I said that, right? But in the spell way, as an incantation, if you want to know. I looked it up on the Internet. And guess what happened?"

"I can't."

"Jeremy. Drank. The. Ink!"

"What ink?"

"The ink on the kitchen bench."

"Why did he drink ink?"

"Because of the spell, you twit."

"Did he know it was ink?"

"I told him it was ink and not to drink it. Then I said the spell in my bedroom, where he couldn't hear me. And he drank it. Against my express instructions."

"Was it in a glass? Or in the ink bottle?"

"I'd put it in an ice-cream sundae glass."

"Maybe he didn't think it was ink?" I was feeling confused. First Polly had told Jeremy not to drink the ink, but then she'd told him to drink it in a spell he couldn't hear. "Maybe he thought you were trying to trick him into not drinking something that was good, by calling it ink? What color was it?"

"Violet," Polly said, "Jane's violet ink. It's very beautiful.

Jeremy's tongue went purple. Probably his pee did, too, but he wouldn't show me."

"Yuck. That's disgusting."

"Anyway, there you are. I think I might be a witch. So I'm going to practice a lot. Jane's having a barbecue tomorrow, and I'm doing a rain spell. I hate barbecues. They just don't cater to vegetarians—I don't care what Jane says about fake sausages."

"But you aren't a vegetarian."

"I am mostly. I'll become a total proper one if I'm a witch. Except for Hawaiian Pizza. It's to do with loving all nature. You can't kill your familiars. Anyway, this isn't solving your father's problem. Let's get down to business."

"If you were really a witch," I said, "then you could just cast a spell for my dad and he'd be fine." A part of me didn't like the idea of Polly being a witch. It gave her a lot of power somehow.

"I'm not that powerful yet," Polly said quickly. "I think against something like depression—which is like an epidemic in today's world—you'd have to be a very experienced witch. I'm just a beginner. No, I think we have to use twenty-first-century remedies for your dad."

"And they are?"

"Well, I asked Marcus if he'd ever been depressed, and he said he was all the time."

That didn't surprise me. Polly's father was an artist.

"So I asked him what he did to get over it," Polly continued, "and he said work, but your dad doesn't have any work, so I asked him what else, and he said love."

"Love?"

"That's right." Polly nodded. "And he must mean Jane, because he's always cursing me and Jeremy—in an interesting way, of course, and not to be taken seriously. So I don't think we can save him from depression. In fact, we probably plunge him into it, more than anything else."

"How can we find Dad love?"

"Easy peasy," Polly said triumphantly. "The Internet, of course!"

"What?"

"Oh, come on, Magenta, everyone's doing it these days. There are newspaper articles all the time—'I Met My Husband on the Internet, Romance on the Web, Finding a Partner Online, Cyberlove.' You can't pretend you haven't heard of online dating!"

"But Dad's too old!"

Polly crossed her arms and looked at me. "My grandma's on Two's Perfect," she said slowly, "and she's talked to lots of guys . . . I mean men. She's had five dates in as many months, and she's in the Really Old bracket."

"I'm sorry," I said. "I didn't realize. I thought it was all . . . you know . . ."

"There are genuinely lonely people out there looking for soul mates."

Polly should have been aiming at advertising as a career rather than changing the world. She could be annoying.

"Okay, okay, forget the guilt trip. How are we going to find my dad an online date when he hates technology these days?"

"Simple." Polly was utterly confident. I stared at her. "We set it up," she said, and spread her arms out wide as though I should have guessed that was all we needed to do.

"I don't get it."

Polly had already moved to her computer, turned it on, and started typing in the password as I spoke. "We log in to an online dating site pretending to be him and then engage some likely partners in conversation."

"So we're matchmaking? On the Internet? For my dad?"

"Yes, that sounds about right."

"It sounds awful," I said, thinking about it. "Polly, it sounds really awful. As though he isn't old enough to make his own decisions. And as though we are. We can't pretend to be him. It's ridiculous. Also it's probably illegal."

"Either this or he goes downhill. That's what is causing his depression, Magenta: it's lack of love. Look at it. When did your mom leave—about three, four years ago? Yes? She's got Trib. Your dad has no one, and he's recently been laid off from his job. He needs someone to love. He's lost it all."

"He's got me," I said indignantly.

"You're around no matter what," Polly said coolly. "You're a given. That doesn't mean you're not important," she added quickly, catching my gaze, "just that you don't necessarily alter the outcome."

"Gee, thanks." I'd hoped she would catch the sarcasm in my tone, but she didn't look up from the keyboard.

"Now we have to create his profile. You know, figure out what makes him attractive to women."

"I don't know. That's kind of disgusting, isn't it?"

"Get your mind out of the gutter, Magenta. It means is he kind to animals? Does he love his children? That kind of thing."

"I don't like it, and I don't think he would, either."

"Well, what are you going to do, then?" Polly asked reasonably. "Wait until he's a basket case and it's too late, or strike while the iron is hot?"

"Okay," I said reluctantly, "what do we write?"

"You're the writer," Polly said. "That's your job."

"You're joking! How would I know what to write?"

"We'll do some research," Polly said, sitting down in the computer chair. "It's got to be simple; thousands and thousands of people do it."

Suddenly we were on an Internet dating site, watching photos of random people popping onto the screen. Some of them were couples with big smiles; others were single, but still smiling. "Meet Melissa or Joe or Bethany," the captions read. "Click here."

"We do a search," Polly said, "for women your dad's age."

"This is tacky," I said, watching her fill in the details. "Really, Polly."

"Are you calling my grandmother tacky?" Polly was too busy typing to be really annoyed.

"No—us doing this is tacky."

She shrugged. "You won't be saying that if we find your dad someone," she said.

"They all more or less say the same thing," I said, reading over her shoulder.

"Then it should be easy to write. You ready?"

Actually it was harder than we expected. Finally we decided that we'd be halfway honest and I'd write up Dad's profile as though he'd asked me to.

"'Decided to get my daughter to write this,'" I wrote. "'After all, she's known me for the longest time anyone has.'"

"What about his mom?" Polly said. "She'd have known him for longer."

"You wouldn't want your mom filling in this kind of stuff," I said.

"Yeah, that's true. What are you going to say?"

"Okay—how does this sound? 'My dad's a terrific friend, always good in a crisis. He's someone you can tell anything to, because he really listens. He's into important things, like saving the planet and gardening. But why don't you see for yourself and contact him?' Do you think I should say something nasty about him so it sounds more real?"

"No, none of the others we've read have. I think it sounds great. Now let's fill in the rest. What kind of music does he like?"

The rest was surprisingly difficult. For a start we just said old music and hoped that would work. I had to skip the book section altogether, because I couldn't remember anything Dad read, except books on World War II, and we both thought that would be against him.

"We can always go back and change it," Polly said, "when we do more research. Plus, we'll need a photo."

"We won't be able to contact anyone," I said after we'd gone back and looked at the rules. "We can't afford to buy these stupid stamps or whatever they are."

"No, we can't, but if someone sees your dad and likes the look of him, she might contact him."

"I don't think this works," I said gloomily. "It's just stupid to think that there are people checking into this every day, hoping they're going to meet someone. I mean, your grandmother's one thing—she's really old. But anyone else? I don't think so."

"Don't you ever read the paper?" Polly asked. "There have been articles on how many people have met online and gotten married. Married!"

"You know I don't read the paper. Anyway, half the stories are exaggerated."

"Look," Polly said, sounding exasperated, "you have to have a little faith, Magenta. You're getting as gloomy as your dad. In fact, you're the one sounding depressed, if you ask me."

"I'm not, honest. I just don't see how—"

"Have some faith," Polly repeated. "Come on, Magenta. Let's look up Love Potions—just in case."

# The Chronicles of Forrdike Castle

By the time I got home from Polly's the next day, it was raining. I was going to call Polly and congratulate her but didn't want the power going to her head. Still, it was uncanny.

"Do you believe in magic?" I asked Dad after breakfast.

"Magic?" Dad repeated. "As in magicians?"

"As in witches."

"That's a tough question. I do think strange things happen that defy logic or science. Perhaps there are people who can focus these events in some way. Of course, in the old days people were called witches just for having some herb lore or healing skills. Mainly women. They burned them at the stake."

A brilliant idea came into my mind. I could include a witch-burning in my novel. Perhaps Lady Rosa would intervene at the last moment. It would add drama. My novel lacked drama.

"Of course, some would argue that women have always been punished for exercising any power . . ."

Dad was still talking. I stifled a yawn and tried to look as though I was paying attention. I could make the witch a little like Polly, I thought. She'd be an apprentice witch, rather than a real one.

"You can look up the Salem witch trials on the Internet," Dad was saying, "and the library would have material on them, too."

"Great," I said, tuning in. It could be useful if I wanted historical accuracy.

"Job day," Dad said, and he sounded a little gloomy. Dad spent Sunday applying for jobs. It was his system. Dad loved systems. He figured they made life work. I didn't think that was necessarily true. I'd overheard Mom telling Trib that Dad even had a system for keeping their marriage together. That clearly hadn't worked.

Back in those days, all Dad's gadgets had beeped and buzzed at regular intervals, keeping his systems intact. These days, of course, he had downsized, and our house was mercifully quiet. He wrote important dates in the Guide Dog Calendar that hung in the kitchen. I suppose that counted as a low-tech system of sorts. He had a high-tech watering system for the veggie garden that involved the bathwater and gutter water. A library-book rotation system that kept the overdue fines at bay, too.

I also had a system. While Dad spent Sunday applying for jobs, I wrote my fantasy novel. I was handwriting it in a great thick notebook my mother gave me. On the front page I had written in my best writing:

*The Chronicles of Forrdike Castle*
*A Fantasy Novel in Three Volumes*
*Volume One*

And on the first page inside I had written the cast of characters:

*Cast of Characters:*
*Rosa Burgundy—sixteen years old and the main character*
*Lady Tamsin—Rosa's mother*
*Lord Burgundy—Rosa's father, missing somewhere in the Southern Isles, presumed dead*
*Lord Treece—Lady Tamsin's paramour*
*Ricardo—Lord Treece's younger brother*
*Echo—Rosa Burgundy's hound and faithful companion*

"Well," I said, "we'd better get busy."

"Still writing the Chronicles? Thinking of putting in a witch?"

"Maybe," I said. "There might be too many pages of description at the moment. I seem to have spent a lot of time describing clothes and things. I need some action."

Dad nodded. I didn't show anyone the Chronicles, especially not my mother. She was an English teacher, and I knew she'd try to correct my grammar and punctuation. Still, I didn't mind talking about them.

Dad sat down at the computer, and I went into my room, retrieved the notebook, and stared at the next blank page. I got up and rearranged the ornaments on my dresser. I went back to my desk. I filled my fountain pen. I had gotten a special fountain pen for Christmas, and I used it all the time for the Chronicles. Dad had bought it because he regarded fountain pens as being sustainable technology, as opposed to ballpoints, which were throwaway consumer items. I liked trying different-colored inks. I had three bottles of ink, but my favorite was an emerald green. I doodled on the blotting paper on my desk. I made some green flowers and some stars. Then I drew a face surrounded by tendrils of curls. I put a tall hat on her, a medieval hat with a wispy veil coming out of the top.

What would I call my witch? I wanted a name that was sort of like Polly and sort of not.

I wandered into the kitchen and opened the fridge door. What would we have for lunch? I wondered.

"Hungry already?" Dad asked. "Magenta, you've just had two muffins."

"I was checking, that's all. I think I have writer's block."

"Ahh," Dad said. "Try a glass of milk."

"Dad! As if. I probably need chocolate."

"There isn't any. Sorry."

"I don't think I can work properly without chocolate."

"Well, Magenta, you might have to do something else, then. I can't go to the store; I'm too busy."

It was no use arguing with him when he used that tone of voice. I sighed heavily so he had to hear me, but then I gave up.

"Polly, Molly, Colly, Holly . . ." Hmm. Holly sounded

good, and it had a plant reference, too. I turned back to the first page and added

Holly—an apprentice witch

to my cast of characters. Then I turned back to the blank page and wrote

Chapter Two

with some curly bits around the C and the T. The first chapter, which had taken me four Sundays, just introduced my central character and her dog. I described the castle in a lot of detail and the three changes of clothes Rosa tried on, in which she was to greet Lord Treece and, more importantly, his younger brother, Ricardo.

Now I had to make her meet him and also meet the young witch, Holly.

"Rosa!" her mother called, and Rosa sighed at her reflection. Perhaps she should have worn the midnight blue after all. The green velvet clung to her as she walked, and the large collar, decorated with thousands of little pearls, framed her heart-shaped face, but did the color make her look a little tired or even— horrors!—a little yellow? "Rosa!" her mother called again. It was clearly too late to change. She would have to do. She swept from the room and started down the main staircase, which led to the entrance hall of the castle. All eyes were on her as she made her way gracefully down. She felt herself blush as she saw Ricardo among the onlookers.

"There you are," her mother said rather peevishly, "at last! Come and greet your stepfather-to-be!"

Rosa held out her white hand and bent her head over a slight curtsy as she had been taught. "Lord Treece," she murmured in her pleasant, low voice.

"Lady Rosa." Lord Treece barely clasped her hand. "You are looking very beautiful today."

"Thank you." Rosa turned to Ricardo but was afraid to look up in case her features betrayed her interest in the young man. "Ricardo." She extended her hand again.

Ricardo grasped it in his and touched it with his mouth. "My lady," he said, "charmed again." His voice was warm.

I won't wash that hand, Rosa thought, not for days.

I wasn't sure that they washed much anyway in the Middle Ages. However, I decided to leave it. I wanted the reader to know how much Rosa was in love with Ricardo.

That made me think of a great idea. What if Rosa seeks Holly out to buy a love potion? That would be a way of introducing the witch. Oh, I was definitely a genius!

The thing I really like about fantasy is that you can put some real life into it without anyone knowing. No one would know that Polly and I had looked at love potions yesterday on the Internet. No one would know that the dashing Ricardo was based, just a little, on Trib's cousin, Richard. Not that I had a crush on Richard. It was just that I liked seeing him. He was funny.

"Show Ricardo around, Rosa. I have made up a room in the West Wing for him and his valet."

"Yes, my lady." Rosa's heart beat so fast she thought she might faint. Her cheeks colored, and she couldn't look at Ricardo but instead inclined her head and began walking toward the passageway that led to the West Wing. Despite her long skirts, she moved fast.

"My lady," Ricardo said, "are you trying to lose me? You might slow down so we can talk. We are to be related in a day or two. We should become better acquainted."

"Yes, my lord." Rosa slowed her pace.

"These are beautiful hangings," Ricardo said, gesturing to the fine tapestries that lined the passageway hanging over the gray stone. "Your mother has fine taste, my lady."

"Thank you, my lord. Actually, my father had them made. Before he went away."

"Before his unfortunate death?" Ricardo asked.

"Before my mother declared him dead," Rosa said, a steely note coming into her voice.

Polly had told me that if someone went missing for long enough, you could legally pronounce them dead and remarry. It was one of her fascinating facts. This had started me thinking about writing the Chronicles. Rosa's father, Lord Burgundy, disappears for years while on a voyage of exploration somewhere. Then her mother, Tamsin Burgundy, meets Lord Treece and falls in love. But in order to marry him, she has to declare Lord Burgundy dead. Rosa hates her for that, of course. She doesn't believe her father is dead. The marriage goes on anyway, and then, at some stage later in the story, Lord Burgundy comes home.

It took a lot of writing to even get Lady Tamsin married. I'd slaved for four Sundays, and she and Lord Treece were no closer to the altar. Which was just as well now that I had a new character to put into the story.

I wrote more about Ricardo and Rosa walking through the castle. I decided that the reader should know what he was wearing, so I gave him some dark knee breeches and a shirt of the softest silk. I wondered if he should have a mustache—or even a little beard. How did men shave in the Middle Ages? Dad had kept his electric shaver, even though he got rid of the microwave. He claimed the electric shaver was the only thing that could get rid of his whiskers. I had argued that the microwave was the only thing that could make popcorn, but then Dad had shown me the old-fashioned way of making it in a saucepan.

Thinking about popcorn made me feel hungry, so I went out to the kitchen again.

"How's it going?" I asked Dad.

"Not bad, not bad at all," Dad said. "There's one job here I wouldn't mind getting."

"That's great, Dad! I hope you get it."

"They probably want someone younger," Dad said. "Everyone does these days." He seemed to be relapsing into pessimism.

"Not necessarily," I said. "You bring experience to the job."

"Employers don't seem to want experience," Dad said. "They want energy and dynamism, neither of which they detect in old codgers like me."

"Dad! Don't get depressed."

"I'm not depressed," Dad said, "just realistic. How are the Chronicles?"

"You know what I think about fantasy? I think fantasy books are always long because the people have to walk everywhere or go on horseback. They can't drive anywhere, so it takes ages to just get them from one place to another. And the castles are big, too. I've just spent hours marching Rosa and Lord Ricardo through the castle to the West Wing. Did castles have wings? I don't even know. I really need to visit a castle. For the atmosphere."

"Right," Dad said. "Start saving your pocket money!"

I rolled my eyes. "As if. The other thing is that you have to keep calling them 'my lady' and 'my lord.' That gets really boring. 'My lady' this and that and the other thing. I wonder if they did that all the time in real life. I'm going to have to do some research."

"Good idea," Dad said. "I bet the library has some excellent books on this kind of thing."

"I'll look it up on the Internet," I said. "No one goes to the library anymore, Dad. That's so last century!"

"As if," Dad said. It was his turn to roll his eyes. At least he didn't sound depressed anymore.

I was always worried on Sundays. As if job day wasn't enough, Sunday was the changing of the guard as well. It was the day I went to Mom's. That was great in some ways. She's got broadband, for a start, and because she's a teacher, I'd have a lot of opportunity to go online and check out any progress on Two's Perfect while she was out. Also she's a more consistent cook than Dad. Dad starts with great intentions, goes to the market, buys strange vegetables or picks some of our spinach, and borrows cookbooks from the library, but he's into improvising. So, for example, if we're out of ordinary potatoes, he'll substitute pumpkin. Cheese, bacon, and pumpkin pie turned out not to be as good as the cheese, bacon, and potato pie from the week before. I'm getting sick of spinach, too. And bitter greens were—guess what—bitter!

I worried about Dad when I wasn't there, too. How did he cope? What did he do all day?

"What do you have going on this week?" I asked. "Anything exciting?"

"Nothing much. Might go and see a movie. What about you?"

"Who would you see a movie with?" I asked, curious.

"You can see movies by yourself, you know," Dad said. "It is allowed."

"But that's so sad," I said. "You wouldn't have anyone to discuss the movie with."

"I don't mind," Dad said.

I knew he was lying. No one likes seeing movies by themselves.

"Oh, Dad," I said, and when we said good-bye at Mom's, I gave him a great big hug and told him I loved him.

"I love you, too, Magenta," he said. "You have a good week, okay?"

"You, too," I said.

"Don't be lonely." I waved until his car turned the corner at the end of the street.

# Happily Ever Afters?

"Congratulations!" Mom threw her arms around me as I stepped through the door. She waved a photocopied page at me. "Great letter, Magenta!"

"Who showed you?" My heart sank. I hadn't expected Mom to see it.

"A girl in my seventh-grade class, of course. They were all huddled around on Friday morning. Then one of the braver ones broke away from the flock and showed me. Great letter, darling. Pity about the subject."

"Well, I am worried, Mom."

"He's fine. I think I do know my ex-husband, Magenta. After all, we managed to live with each other for fifteen years. I probably know him better than anyone else in the world, given that his father is some introverted eccentric up the North Coast and his mother is dead. He's fine. Not finding a job, of course, but other than that, fine."

"The market's tight," I said, repeating what Dad had told me. I clenched my hands in my jeans pockets. I hated it when Mom talked about all this.

"Trib has managed to find three jobs in the time it's taken your father to find none."

"Trib is younger than you and Dad," I said smoothly and then held my breath. Mom just gave me a look that said it all—a flash of anger followed by a cloud of disappointment with an edge of anxiety. Actually, to be fair, Trib wasn't that much younger. It was just useful ammunition when she overstepped the boundary into Dad's life with me. It shook her up. I thought of it as Mom's time-out.

She visibly relaxed her face. "I'm sorry," she said. "I just worry when you worry about Max. You shouldn't have to, and then that makes me mad that he's letting you."

"He doesn't want me to worry, either," I said warily.

"Well, then, why doesn't he do something about it?" Mom glared at me. "God, he could get a telemarketing job or something."

"Mom!" She knew this was out of bounds. She just knew it.

"I'm the one paying child support, Magenta!"

"Tell someone else, not me," I said, and pushed past her to my bedroom, feeling the tears prickle at the back of my eyes. It wasn't Dad's fault. When Mom had left him, I'd first gone with her and seen Dad every second weekend. Then he got laid off and put all his severance package into a small house with a reasonable-size yard that got a little sun. That was pretty important up where we live if you plan to grow veggies. Every second weekend we dug the duck pond and prepared the garden.

When Mom met Trib, she had one of her meltdowns.

She stormed at Dad the next time she saw him and said that she had no time of her own and did he know what teaching was like these days and how could she manage to parent me 98 percent of the time, maintain her professional standing 100 percent, and attempt to be in a new relationship as well? Something had to give, she said, and it wasn't going to be her profession and it wasn't going to be her new relationship, because after all, she deserved that, didn't she?

So it was me.

All that sounds much harsher than it was meant, by the way. My mother has been teaching for nearly twenty years, and she knows how to use her emotions to get exactly the behavior she wants. Except this time it didn't work. She'd wanted a couple of extra nights off without me—I knew because she'd discussed it with me. She and Trib just needed a bit of extra child-free time to get to know each other.

Instead my dad totally agreed with her and arranged to get me every alternate week. That was fine, until she realized she'd have to give him child-support payments. Then everything hit the roof again.

You can push Dad and you can push him, but when he reaches his limit, he is immovable. A mountain. I know.

"You got what you wanted," he told Mom. I remember we were standing on her veranda and she was screaming at him. He held my hands warmly between his own two big ones and hugged me against him with his free arm.

"You'll leave me destitute!" I remember that word because I'd only just found out what it meant, and I couldn't imagine it happening to my mother.

"Hardly." He smiled. "I think you'll find the government

is reluctant to take more than they think people can afford. Get a good accountant on it, Tammy. That will probably ease some of the burden."

"I won't do anything dishonest."

"Did I say you should?"

I should say that this was a stage of their divorce that was less than friendly. I didn't understand and actually wasn't even meant to hear what was said. But I eavesdropped, because it was my life, too, and I hated the way they thought it had nothing to do with me. Or rather, I eavesdropped until it made me too angry or frustrated or sad, and then I'd plug in my MP3 player and play music.

So, anyway, Mom does pay Dad child support, and I live with Dad every alternate week. The duck pond is finished. We had a bit of landslide trouble back in the heavy summer rain, but it's looking okay now. We just haven't got the ducks yet. The veggie garden's looking good, though. And Mom's relationship with Trib flourished to the point that they are getting married in a few months' time. That's probably why the discussion has gone back to Dad's failure to get a job. Weddings, as Mom keeps saying, are expensive.

Apart from the financial flare-ups, I don't mind living in two places. I imagine I will later when I've got heaps and heaps of homework to do and a bag that's bigger than me, but for the time being, it's pretty cool. I almost get to be two different Magentas.

"You're breaking the rules," I told Mom, stuck my fingers in my ears, and shut my bedroom door behind me. Everything here was neat. I had a bookcase-wardrobe-bunk-bed unit that Mom had put together for me and that

I had painted a deep green. My room had a forest theme. On the wall around my chest of drawers, Trib had helped draw me a huge tree with vines looped through the branches. It had taken us six months to get it absolutely right. Trib was patient with things like that, though. He said it was good therapy. Mom and I had painted the trees and some huge yet-to-be-discovered vine flowers that glowed in different colors. I had a collection of rocks piled up on top of another bookcase that held my fantasy reference material.

It was the ideal room for Magenta, teenage fantasy writer.

I threw myself down on the bed and pulled all the scatter cushions around me until I was walled in with pillowed softness. My favorite cushion had a tapestry picture of a great antlered stag on it. Mom had made it for me, and she was now making me one of a young woman dressed in medieval costume with a thin hunting dog at her feet. That was my dog—my fantasy dog, Echo.

I expected Mom to follow me and began counting in my head. Usually I only got up to a hundred before my door opened and Mom came in to apologize. This time, though, the phone rang, and so it took up to five hundred.

She sat on the end of my bed and stroked my ankle carefully. I held a cushion to my face so I couldn't see all of her. She stroked for a while in silence, up and down along my foot and then up to my ankle again. It almost, but not quite, tickled.

"I'm sorry," she said eventually. "Grown-up life gets a bit tricky, you know. But you are absolutely right, I shouldn't talk about it to you or in front of you. It's just that you're the only person I know who sees him and knows what's going on on his end.

"Then this problem-page letter of yours! I'm only worried, Magenta. Just because you leave someone doesn't mean that you stop worrying about them."

"You're worried about money," I said in the tightest, meanest voice I could manage. I had to move the cushion and say it all again because it muffled my first attempt.

"True," she admitted. "There are things Trib and I would like to do, and they require a bit more money than I have available at the moment. But I am also worried about your father. It may not always sound that way, but that's the way it is."

"Just don't talk to me about it."

"Magenta," she said, and I could hear an edge creeping into her voice, "I do try not to. Then my seventh-grade girls show me a letter that has clearly been written by you and sent into a public forum. A public forum. So now I am worried about you worrying about your father. Clearly you are the innocent party in all this, so I'm not only worried about you, I'm angry that your father has made me have to be. I know this may not make sense to you. At the same time, I'm kind of proud you wrote the letter and doubly proud that it was such a good letter."

There was silence while we both struggled not to cry. Through the far edge of the pillow, I could see she had pressed her fingers against her eyes as though to hold the tears inside. She's good at that. When I try it, the tears spill around my fingers, so I swallow hard and screw my face up. That was a good reason for keeping the cushion over it!

"Okay," she said eventually, "let's start again. Magenta, it's great to see you, and congratulations on the very fine letter that you've recently had published."

"Thank you, Mom. I wasn't going to show you due to the subject matter, but I'm pleased it has been brought to your attention."

"That phone call was from Trib. He's been held up in Sydney, so we'll have a girls' night. Just the two of us. What do you think?"

"A DVD?"

"Oh, definitely with a DVD. And, if you wouldn't mind, I'd love to have my nails done."

"That would be a pleasure, Lady Tammy. Perhaps I could request a similar service?"

"Delighted. A foot soak, too, might refresh us? Not to mention some delicious morsels—chips and dip, or something more substantial?"

"Pizza from the Gourmet to Go? There are, after all, only two of us."

"Gourmet to Go it is."

Mom and I settled down with a roast pumpkin, feta, and pine-nut pizza with pesto sauce and watched ditzy-blonde movies most of the night. She had another call from Trib, and I had one from Polly. She took the call from Trib into her room, and I paused the DVD. So when Polly called me, I insisted on the DVD being paused and taking the call in my room, too.

"It's up!" Polly said.

"What? Oh, and congratulations on the rain, by the way."

"It was nothing." I could hear Polly's smile in her voice. "A little wet rhyme." She laughed maniacally at her own lame joke. "No, the real thing is that the profile is up on Two's Perfect. It reads pretty well. I added some stuff after you left, to make him sound like more of a catch. I checked with Nanna. She said everyone wants to sound better than they actually are, and you take the profiles with a bucketload, never mind a pinch, of salt."

"How can I see it?"

"Could you go on at your mom's place?"

"Too risky. Trib's been held up in Sydney, so she might get prowly."

"Okay, tomorrow at my place after school. We've still got some information to fill in. And a photo. We desperately need a photo. I don't think we'll get any hits until we have a photo up. People will think he's gross or something. With bad skin disease. Or a huge hump. It's superficial, but the dating marketplace is. You just have to face the facts."

I could always tell when Polly had been talking to her grandmother. She just repeated huge chunks of their conversation without changing a word. I thought it might be plagiarism, but according to Polly, you couldn't plagiarize direct speech. That was really a good thing for a writer, I thought. It even helped me a little, although my characters had to talk weirdly because of the age they lived in, so it was more difficult for me. I mean, as an example, how do you translate this sentence I overheard on the train into the Middle Ages? "We had such a totally, like, awesome night with these random dudes we met on MySpace." I'd have to write, "The feast was splendid, and I enjoyed the unexpected company of my lord Harry and the rest of his hunting party, who had fortuitously stumbled across our smallholding on their way to . . ." You get the picture. No wonder fantasy books never come singly. You can't learn the language in just one book. Babbling on like that takes up so much space.

I'd be writing the Chronicles while I was in college at this rate. If I get into college and don't fail school because of all the time the Chronicles are taking out of my life. I'm certainly never going to manage a boyfriend.

"Okay—I'll clear it with Mom. But she'll be fine. See you at school."

The DVD ended just as we knew it would. The couple got married and lived happily ever after.

"For seven and a half years," Mom said.

"What?"

"The national average length of a marriage these days."

I shook my head. "Why bother?" I asked. Marriage seemed a bit like writing a fantasy novel to me—but apparently you didn't get to write a trilogy. Unless, of course, that was why people tried again.

"Do you think marrying Trib is like having another go at the story?" I asked Mom as we brushed our teeth together.

"What?" She spluttered toothpaste everywhere. "What do you mean?"

"Well, like fantasy. You've got the language and the characters and a little of the plot, so you start the first book, but it doesn't work out. You've still got the language, and you've introduced a new character, and you've got your plot that could maybe still work?"

"Magenta McPhee, I think that is the most brilliant definition of a second marriage I've ever heard. Chilling, but brilliant. Go and write it down somewhere. When you're a world-famous fantasy writer, you can sell your juvenilia to some rich university library."

"Do people do that?"

"All the time." Mom nodded. "Keep everything!"

I did write it in my journal. My everyday journal. I added some biting comments on the plight of a child caught in the cross fire of financial strife, but I added that Mom and I had had a really good girls' night in and that my face felt as soft as rose petals after using Mom's new face mask. I didn't want anyone from a university thinking I had issues with my mom. We got along fine . . . when she left Dad out of it.

I was woken in the morning by my cell phone. It was Polly sending me a text. She had a cell she used only in the strictest of emergencies, as she didn't approve of them. It was a short message.

*Bring photo of yr dad.*

A photo! That was going to be difficult. I could hardly ask Mom, particularly not after last night. I told Mom I'd walk to school, rather than get a lift, and she told me that Trib might not be home tonight either, and that after she picked me up from Polly's, we could look through the wedding plans if I wanted. Great, I thought, more wedding plans. But I tried to look enthusiastic instead and waved good-bye.

Then I went photo hunting.

Mom didn't have any, of course. There were none in my room, either. I kept photos of Mom and me at her place and of Dad and me at Dad's place. I checked the storeroom. Buried underneath some old magazines was a big wedding album. I flipped through it. It's funny, but at weddings they only take photos of the bride by herself, never the groom. Also, you'd have been able to tell it was a wedding because Dad was in a suit with a funny bow tie. Plus, he was years and years younger. They wouldn't do at all.

Then I found a falling-apart photo album from a holiday we took—the last holiday together. Okay, Dad was still a fair bit younger than he looked now, and Mom was in it, but they were separated by me, and I thought I might just manage to cut Dad out of the photo. Maybe.

I peeled the photo off and put it carefully between pages in my planner and then had to almost run the whole way to school to make it before the bell rang.

In the end we cut just Mom out and left me in, because Polly said the photo with me looked as though Dad was a good family man. Also it was harder to cut me out because he had his arm on my shoulders (but not around Mom's, I couldn't help noticing). We scanned the photo and then loaded it onto Dad's profile.

"I added some stuff," Polly said sheepishly. "I thought he didn't sound romantic enough."

She'd added, "Well, that was my daughter speaking,

and I second her thoughts but decided I should add that I'm looking for that special someone. Someone I can walk on beaches with, cuddle up in front of fires with, look for falling stars with, and tell my secrets to. I love camping out—being at one with nature. I love reading a good book, watching a good movie, and listening to good music—but all that is empty without a special someone to talk things over with."

"You should be a writer," I said sarcastically.

"Do you think so?" Polly asked. "I thought it was pretty good, but I really want to do environmental science."

"I was joking. I think it sounds stupid and just like every other desperate person here."

"You're just jealous, Magenta McPhee!"

"I'm not," I said. "You're just a third-rate romance writer, Polly Davies."

"I am not!"

But we posted it anyway, with the photo. Then Polly did a kind of spell thing. She called it a finding spell, but she'd just made it up, I could tell. The incense she waved at the computer wasn't particularly convincing, either.

"Looking, looking, always looking, I need a time that's ripe for cooking. Finding, finding—that be joy. A pretty girl for this lonely boy."

"That's so lame, Polly," I said, and would have said more, but at that moment Jane came in.

"What on earth's that smell? Not that gruesome incense again, Polly? It will taint my kitchen, darling. Hello, Magenta, lovely to see you! How are things?" Jane swept in, waving her arms at the wisps of incense smoke. "Do open a window, Polly. Staying for tea, Magenta? Had a cancellation—so we've got Moroccan snack packs—spicy lamb, tabbouleh with preserved lemon, and a wedge of Turkish bread served with an eggplant relish. Fifty servings beautifully packaged in the Green Box signature recycled cardboard box, each with 'Happy Ever After' written on them. I wrote fifty 'Happy Ever Afters' in the early hours this morning. It was an engagement party."

"What happened?" I had wondered why Jane looked a little bedraggled around her designer edges.

"She got a text message from an old boyfriend. A text message! All my work. And I can't freeze it. Eggplant deteriorates. We just have to eat Moroccan packs until they're gone. Do stay for dinner, Magenta. Would your mother be free, do you think? And what about that boyfriend of hers—Tib?"

"Trib," I said. "No, he's in Sydney fixing a network, but Mom might be able to come. Do you want me to call her?"

"Yes, please do. That would be, let's see, three packs for Marcus, two for the rest of us. . . . They're very small servings, just a light, slightly-more-than-finger-food, less-than-dinner, not-quite-lunch sort of thing to serve with drinks. That would be eleven gone already. Maybe four for Marcus, three for the rest of us. Gosh, that would only leave me with thirty-four. Then you could take home—say, ten? I could give ten to dear Amanda, and we'd only have to eat fourteen more! Just think, Polly, only three days of Moroccan nights."

I loved Jane. She always managed to turn a potential

disaster into a good thing. Plus, she's the coolest-looking mom. She has dead black hair with these bright red wings at the sides. They go with her eyeglass rims and her lipstick. Her hair's as short as a boy's so she doesn't have to put it up in the kitchen, she says, but Polly says it's because she likes to show off her neck. Marcus has made her neck into a sculpture. It's one of his not-quite-famous sculptures bought by a regional gallery. A very prominent regional gallery, Jane says. But Marcus just sniffs.

So we all ate Moroccan packs for dinner from little cardboard boxes. I saved one of my boxes. I liked the idea of having a Happy Ever After box. I wasn't sure what I could do with it, but I knew it would come in handy for something. And even if it didn't, it was good to have something that believed in Happy Ever Afters.

# Spooky

Trib came home in the middle of the week, and that put an end to chick-flick DVDs and takeout. Mom went back to trying to be a domestic goddess, and I decided to try to get Lady Rosa to the wedding. My readers wouldn't be all that interested in how Ricardo shaved, but they'd probably enjoy hearing about Lady Tamsin and Rosa's wedding clothes. Lady Tamsin would have to look spectacular, so I dressed her in a golden gown covered in seed pearls. In contrast, Rosa wore a pale green gown, the color of new leaves. I was a bit stumped when it came to what they'd eat. I decided that roast suckling pig sounded just the thing. I put an apple in its mouth for good measure. How you could eat anything that still had a face was beyond me. It was enough to turn me vegetarian. Polly agreed.

"It's disgusting," she said on the phone. "Pigs squeal when they're about to be slaughtered."

"How do you know?" My pig would have to have been killed in the castle grounds. Mind you, it would be kind of interesting if Rosa heard it and refused to eat it. But then what would she get to eat? I wasn't sure that there were a lot of vegetables around in those days.

"Cabbage, turnips, carrots," Polly suggested, "and she could always fill up with bread."

In the end I let her have a ladylike shudder at the pig's head, but Ricardo, always a gentleman, carves her a succulent slice.

"You must eat, my Lady Rosa; your skin is as pale as starlight. Becoming, of course, but perhaps this piece of succulent pork will bring a slight blush of dawn to your face."

Ricardo was the bee's knees as far as I was concerned!

"Thank you, my lord. Your compliments are as gratefully received as the food you heap on my plate."

"My compliments fade in comparison to their subject, madam!" Lord Ricardo bowed low over the plate he proffered.

Really, it was hard to imagine how they were actually ever going to kiss, given that they had to talk in this extremely fancy way. I'd have to introduce Holly quickly. This wedding feast just ended up making me hungry.

Mom was preparing roast lamb and veggies in the kitchen. Her face was all sweaty because the oven was on, and she had streaks of flour over her black top, despite the apron she wore.

"Don't eat too much," she warned. "Dinner will be in an hour or so."

"An hour is ages away, Mom. I'm starving." I wolfed down two more cookies while her back was turned. "What kind of food do you think you'll have when you and Trib get married?"

"Well," Mom said, giving me complete attention, "I wondered if Jane wouldn't cater it, given that it will be very small. I did love the Moroccan Nights idea—though I'm not sure about making that a wedding theme, to be quite honest. I can't see myself wearing harem pants. They're so seventies. Then I wondered about a kind of picnic thing. Jane could put together little picnic baskets. But then, why ask Jane to do that? I could put 'BYO picnic basket' on the invitation. We want to keep the cost down."

"You could have suckling pig," I suggested, "with an apple in its mouth. A kind of medieval theme. We could wear costumes. Trib would look dashing in breeches."

"Tights," Mom said. "The men wore tights."

"Oh, no, I'll have to rewrite everything. I thought they wore breeches."

"Well, no, darling, kirtles and hose. Don't you love the word *kirtle*?"

"Oh, dear," I said, "I really do have to do some research, don't I?"

"I expect you do. Anyway, I don't think a medieval theme is the way to go for us. We want something simple. Simple but elegant. Or simple but chic, even if it's slightly shabby chic."

I had no idea what she was talking about, so I just nodded and scarfed another cookie while she arranged things in the oven.

"I need some action," I told her when I had her attention again, "for the Chronicles. Things aren't happening fast enough. I'm going to introduce an apprentice witch, but I'm not sure that will be enough."

"She could kill someone," she suggested, "or try to. That's even better."

"I need some action," I told Trib over dinner, "for the Chronicles."

"A car chase," Trib suggested. He was catching up on reading the papers, even though I couldn't read at the table.

"It's set in the Middle Ages," I said, "so I don't think a car chase is exactly what I need."

Mom spluttered. "It'd be action, though," she said. "You could add some time travel—a *Dr. Who* kind of thing. They could arrive in a blue Chevrolet, right smack in the middle of the wedding. That would be action for you!"

"Not the kind I'm looking for. Thank you all the same." I hated the way she sometimes took the Chronicles seriously and sometimes, especially when Trib was around, treated them as if they were a big joke. She must have caught my expression.

"Lots of writers do that kind of time travel these days. Honestly, it can be interesting, Magenta."

"I'm writing a purer kind of fantasy," I said in my best posh voice, "more traditional."

"Horse chase," Trib said. "You know, knights on horseback chasing each other all over the countryside. Or a joust, and the bad guy wins and there's revolution in the air."

"I think I should ask people more familiar with the genre," I said, and left the table as haughtily as I possibly could, given that I'd spilled a splotch of gravy on my white T-shirt.

"I need some action," I said to Polly. "It's not going well. When you're bored writing it, how could a reader be interested?"

"A rival for Rosa's affections," Polly said, "that's what you need. Or crank up the unresolved sexual tension."

"The what?"

"Unresolved sexual tension. It's what Marcus says fuels contemporary television drama."

"Yeah, but what is it?"

"I think it's where two people want to kiss—and more—but never quite end up doing it. It's everywhere."

"I'm trying to do that," I told her, "but it's hard when they have to talk in such big sentences. They never really get around to saying anything. It's frustrating."

"Well, can't you just have them cut to the chase? I mean, they must have at some stage in the Middle Ages, or the human race would have died out."

"There's reality, Polly, and then there's fictional reality," I said, copying what our English teacher had told us. "I'm dealing with fiction, and it's frustrating."

"Hey! Oh, Magenta, turn on your computer. Check it out! Your dad's got mail!"

"What?"

"Someone e-mailed him!"

"Who? Who?" I was busy turning on the computer as I spoke.

"She's forty-two, one son, interested in outdoor things and the environment, blah, blah—they all say that—is home-centered. What does that mean? But likes to eat out, listen to live music, and see movies. Though she's equally at peace—at peace, that's a bit lame—eating takeout and watching a DVD."

I'd brought up the site by this stage and found Dad's profile, and sure enough, there was the e-mail. "Her name's Spookylianna," I said. "That's just weird, Polly. Why would anyone call themselves that?"

"Search me. She looks pretty ordinary in the photo."

It was true. She looked like an ordinary, middle-aged kind of woman. She was smiling so hard that her eyes were all crinkly at the corners. But at least she was smiling.

"What should we do now?"

"We'll have to e-mail her back," Polly said, "and chat. That's what people do. Look—she's even given him her e-mail address. I don't think you're supposed to do that. That's great, Magenta. It means she must be really interested."

"What will we talk about?"

"Well, what do people talk about?" Polly said.

"I don't know." I was suddenly frozen. What did people talk about? Lady Rosa and Ricardo paid each other compliments. Mom and Trib talked about the wedding. Dad and I talked about school, and he talked about current events. None of that seemed appropriate.

"Jane and Marcus talk about finances, the weather, the garden, and how smart Jeremy is. They don't talk about me at all. Or not when I can hear them."

"I don't think that's helpful," I told her.

"Yes, it is," Polly said. "Your dad could talk about you, the weather, and the veggie garden. I think I've been extremely helpful. I don't think you're being very positive, Magenta."

"Sorry. Okay—I'll try. So . . . 'Dear Spookylianna, It was lovely to hear from you. You sound like a very interesting person, and I think we may have some common interests. How old is your son? What is he interested in? My daughter's interested in fantasy, writing, and shopping. She's bad at math but gets top grades in English. She's started high school. She spends every other week at her mom's place.' "

"I don't think it should be quite so much about you," Polly said.

"But you said to talk about me."

"I didn't mean take up the whole e-mail with you!"

"Okay—what if I add something about the veggies?"

In the end we got something that sounded as though an adult had written it, pretty boring if you asked me, but Polly felt it was the kind of e-mail Spooky would expect. Before we could change anything again, I pushed the Send button.

"Hey, Magenta!" Mom called. "Richard's here—don't you want to say hello?"

"Oh, my God, Polly," I whispered, "Ricardo's—I mean Richard's here. I've got to go. I have to change. I've got gravy on my T-shirt."

"Break a leg," Polly said ambiguously, and hung up right away.

"I'll be out in a sec," I called out, noticing how my voice went all high and quavery. How girly. I was appalled. I quickly pulled on a clean black T-shirt to counteract the voice effect. I pulled my hair out of its ponytail and swiped some gloss over my mouth. "Hi, Richard," I said into the mirror, lowering my voice and trying to look mysteriously at my own reflection through my eyelashes. It cricked my neck slightly and made me look oddly cross-eyed, but the voice was okay.

"Magenta!" Mom came to the doorway. "Hurry up. What are you doing?"

"Nothing, just hanging up the phone."

"Well, come on, he's just dropping some stuff off."

I followed Mom into the living room. Richard was slouched down on one of the chairs, drinking a beer with Trib.

"Hey, it's Magwheels. How are you, gorgeous?"

"Hi, Richard." My voice didn't sound husky and deep, but it didn't quite squeak. Gorgeous, he called me gorgeous. Thank God for the little black T-Shirt! "Pretty good. And you?"

"Same old. Still writing?"

"Yeah." I shrugged. "It's slow, you know. My latest theory is that fantasy is about a hundred times slower than other writing because people have to walk everywhere."

"Good thinking," he said. "So why don't you introduce an air machine or something? Like an airship—you know, anime-style. That'd rock."

I shook my head. "I'm a traditionalist. I don't want to mess with form."

"I said she should do a car chase," Trib offered, and the two guys guffawed for a while.

"Sorry," Richard said, finally noticing my exaggerated sighs and finger tapping. "Shouldn't tease the workers. Hey, I didn't forget you, Magenta. Close your eyes, and hold out your hand."

I did as I was told. He dropped something smooth, cold, and egg-shaped into my hand. It was heavy.

"Open them."

He'd given me a rock: an egg-shaped, egg-sized, smooth, orangey rock. It was a like a dragon's egg. It grew warmer as I held it.

"From the desert," he said. "I saw it when the bus stopped, and everyone thought I was crazy, but I knew you had to have it, Magenta."

"Thanks, Richard."

"I got you something else, too, just in case you thought a rock was kind of a cheap present. Here, hold out your wrist." He fastened a little bracelet made of shells around my wrist.

"Wow! Richard!" I gave him a clumsy one-arm hug. He smelled great. I closed my eyes for a millisecond, just breathing the smell of him in. Some kind of cologne, a bit of honest sweat, and the smell of new sheets that have dried in the sun. Oh, Ricardo!

"Hey, little cuz, it's okay. Glad you like them."

"I love them," I said, and my voice squeaked again. Damn! Should practice "husky" more often.

Then some current-affairs program came on TV, and he and Trib turned to it while Mom went into the kitchen to make herbal tea.

I sat on the couch as close to Richard as I could get without being obvious. I pretended to watch TV, but I was really admiring my new bracelet while I held my rock egg. The egg he'd brought for me, back from the desert. The one he'd seen and thought of me, all those miles—nearly two states—away. He'd risked ridicule picking it up and keeping it. For me.

"Well," he said when the program finished, "better go. Good to see you all again. Bye, Tammy. Bye, Trib. Bye, Magwheels."

"Come for dinner next time," Mom said. "Come for pizza or even a home-cooked roast lamb."

We waved him good-bye.

"He's so thoughtful," Mom said to Trib. "Honestly, he needn't have bought me anything." Richard had given her some shell-shaped soaps in a little bag dyed ocean colors. I had my eye on the bag. I could use it for my cell phone.

"He's a big kid who likes to shop," Trib said. "Plus he likes you. He's a good kid. My sis did one thing right."

I slept that night with the egg-rock under my pillow. It was a bit lumpy, but I moved it until it was under the part of the pillow I squash up. I wanted to keep it warm all night.

The next morning, before I'd even had breakfast, I e-mailed Polly about the rock egg and the bracelet, and then I thought I'd better check Dad's Hotmail account in case Spooky had e-mailed him. I didn't think she would have. After all, you're supposed to move slowly into these things, but she was obviously the go-getter type. There wasn't just one e-mail from her, there were two.

Dear Greenman, (That was Polly's idea, not mine!)

Wow! I hadn't expected a reply so soon. Or such a long e-mail. I mean, most guys think that three lines is a lot of effort. I'll try to answer your questions, and then I'll throw some of mine into the ring, shall I?

My son is fourteen. It's a difficult age. He's a great kid who's had to deal with a lot of stuff, and I'm very proud of him. He's not a standard-issue kind of boy. He's pretty quiet, maybe even a bit nerdy, but he's been a fabulous support for me over the years. He's got a lot of interests, including computer games, and he reads a lot. He could do with a male mentor, though. I'm afraid my ex isn't very helpful in that regard, as he doesn't see Cal very often.

I do a few things. I'm involved in some community groups and help out a friend who has a café from time to time. I've been basically in recovery from some unpleasant relationship issues for a while. But I can feel myself becoming whole again. Didn't someone once say what doesn't kill us makes us stronger?

I'm thinking of studying to become a masseuse. I like the idea of earning money doing something that heals others.

I do envy your veggie garden. Unfortunately, the house we're renting has this really vertical kind of garden. I think you could terrace it or something, but not when you're renting.

And how wonderful to go camping with your daughter. See, I think that's the kind of thing Cal needs—just to give him some other outlets. He needs to really witness nature, not just the inside of his bedroom. But camping's not the kind of thing I'd feel confident doing by myself. Being a single woman cuts off a lot of things that I'd normally love doing.

How about you? Do you love traveling? What kind of music do you listen to? Are you into meditation?

Let's keep talking,<br>Lianna

Then the second e-mail said:

Dear Greenman,

Sorry, just realized how much I'd written. I hope you don't find it boring. It's so easy to run on in an e-mail, isn't it? You just sit down in from of the keyboard and find yourself saying things you probably wouldn't say in person. I'd be intimidated. Or think they sounded weird. Hope you don't mind these long e-mails. I'll try to keep them shorter in the future.

Lianna

I printed them out and took them to school. We were in way over our heads, I thought. Polly disagreed.

"She sounds okay," she said. "A bit wacky, but not totally off the planet."

"She talks about healing too much, and issues," I said.

"Yeah, but she's opening up. We'd better make your dad open up, too."

"What?"

"You know, show his vulnerable side."

"Which is?"

"I dunno. It's too early to say he's unemployed, isn't it?"

"Dad always says self-employed when he applies for a job." Polly was the only person I could tell this kind of stuff to.

"Yeah, good thinking. Do you want me to, you know, try casting a get-a-job spell for him?"

I practically swiveled my head so I could stare Polly right in the face. She stared back unflinchingly. "You think you can do that?"

"I just need a bit of his hair."

"A bit of his hair?"

"To do the spell."

"Okay, well, I'll see what I can do. I guess."

"They're working. I tell you, Mags, they're working. Last night I cast a finding spell, and Jane found this locket she hasn't been able to find for the past year. She was overjoyed."

"So did you tell her?"

"That I'm a witch? Are you crazy? Of course not. She'd go bonkers. Jane's not into the occult. Her deepest mystery is puff pastry."

"Surely Marcus would understand?"

"Marcus is so self-obsessed that he only understands his

own ego," Polly said. "I'm telling you, he'd better be the genius Jane thinks he is, or she's in for a disappointed old age."

"Are things okay?" I asked hesitantly. Polly could be sharp with her family, but this sounded bitter.

"Yeah, fine. Witches shouldn't be thanked for their work, not unless someone approaches them directly. I'm still in the apprentice stage, of course, so no one's likely to approach me. Except you. And I know you'll thank me, Magenta."

"Yeah, well, of course. If Dad gets a job, I'll credit you. Absolutely."

"Thanks, Magenta. Best friends for life?"

"Best friends for life," I said, and we pinky-hugged.

"We'd better get that e-mail written, then," Polly said, pulling away and settling her laptop on her knee in a businesslike manner.

That took the rest of the lunch. I'd thought writing fantasy was hard, but that was just making stuff up. Writing Dad's e-mails was much more difficult. It had to really sound like him. But a different kind of him. The him that this Lianna might really like.

"Sort of gentle but manly, supportive but not demanding, interesting but interested," Polly said. "The perfect listener, but someone who's not afraid to speak up as well."

"How do you know this kind of stuff?"

"Jane reads magazines and romances. She says they help stop her from cooking in her dreams. But I figure it's because Marcus is so removed. From us, anyway. He's there for Jeremy. Jeremy only needs to fart, and he's got Marcus's complete attention. Jane and I could be on fire, and he'd put the finishing touches on whatever he was working on before he'd pick up the bucket of water."

"Did you guys have a fight?"

"Not a fight, exactly. The other person has to be around to have a fight. I'm just not talking to him. Can we get on with the e-mail?"

"Okay, let's work on one aspect at a time. Let's start with answering her questions."

I was proud of the return e-mail. We kept it reasonably short—to fit in with Spooky's expectations. We cut out an *awesome* that crept in and said *great* instead. *Great* sounded more grown-up. And Polly made me cut most of my questions about Cal. I must admit I was quite intrigued by him. Although my passion for Richard is undying, I could do with some practice in boy/girl stuff.

"I'll type it up and send it tonight," I said. "I hope she takes her time in replying to this one. Doesn't she know you shouldn't be too eager? I just don't want to spend all my lunchtimes writing e-mails from my dad. It's hard work, Polly."

"I know. Eventually, of course, they'll have to meet. But wait until they get to know each other better."

"You mean wait until she gets to know what we think he's like with other adults and *we* get to know *her* better."

"That sounds like math," Polly said, "but I think you're probably right."

"All my creative energy is going into this," I said. "I'll

probably be too exhausted to write the Chronicles tonight and have to do homework instead."

"What about my spells?"

"They're just little poems, Polly, not like a whole big book."

"Just as hard to write. You have to rhyme."

I looked at her and decided not to argue. When Polly gets upset, she gets little white patches near her mouth, as though she's holding it too tightly or maybe biting it from the inside. When I see that look, I try to stop. Polly can be upset for days, and I really needed her to help with the e-mails.

I sent Dad's latest off that evening and didn't dare look at his e-mail before I finally got to sleep after completing the week's math homework. I had a horrible feeling that Spooky might already have written him back. Well, I was going to save her from herself. I was going to pretend she wasn't as eager as she seemed to be.

I held off looking until Saturday morning, when Trib and Mom went out wedding shopping. They don't really call it wedding shopping. That's what I call it. What they do is get in the car and drive to some café where Mom orders a latte and Trib has a macchiato. Mom reads the café magazines while Trib looks over the paper. Then, eventually, Mom comes up with a different wedding idea— based on something she's seen. And they discuss it through another coffee. I went with them once, and it was so boring. Honestly, the ideas my mom can get from a piece of orange-and-almond cake.

"We could have a kind of spring theme," she said. "You know, everything yellow and cream."

"Yes, I see what you mean." Trib had ordered lemon cheesecake.

"You could have a chocolate theme," I said, hoeing into a slice of rich mud cake. "You know, you could both wear dark brown, and the wedding cake could be chocolate. A bit like this." I held up a piece to show them, but unfortunately it broke and smudged the clean white tablecloth. Mom sighed, and Trib looked away. So I knew it wasn't going to be a chocolate wedding.

I took the opportunity to call Polly and open Dad's e-mail.

"She's replied," I said.

"Of course she has. It's been two days, Mags. Didn't you check it yesterday?"

"Nah. Or the day before. I thought I'd give her a chance to slow down."

"What does she say?"

"Well, she wants to know what Max is short for, and then there's a lot of stuff about him being understanding because he's obviously gone through rough times. It's all pretty boring. This is getting harder and harder."

"Oh, stop whining," Polly said sharply. "You should be grateful your dad is actually talking to someone. More than what's going on here."

"But he isn't," I said. "My dad isn't—I am. And it's taking up a lot of my time."

"At least it's short-term. I figure a couple more e-mails and we can ask her to meet him."

"Right." On the one hand, this was good, since I could stop faking it. On the other hand, I'd have to admit to Dad I had been pretending to be him to some strange woman who called herself Spookylianna. I wasn't sure that Dad would be thrilled about being Greenman, either.

It took me hours and several rounds of toast with Nutella to write Dad's e-mail back. When I'd finished, I couldn't bear to look at the Chronicles. On the plus side, math looked relatively easy. You didn't have to worry about anyone's feelings. The numbers worked or they didn't. It was that simple.

"We've got it!" Mom rushed through the door as I'd finished working out the circumferences. "We're going to have a garden party."

"A garden party? Oh, you mean a garden-party wedding?"

"Yes." Trib beamed. "We had a vision."

"A vision?" It was all a little sudden after circumferences.

"Hats," Mom said, "hats and ribbon sandwiches on a trestle table covered with a white cloth. A heavy white cloth, not a sheet, Trib. A vase of pink roses tumbling down in the center, trailing around a tiered cake plate covered in cupcakes. I'll wear a floaty skirt and top—nothing too formal. Trib can wear jeans and some kind of pale shirt."

"A trendy shirt," Trib said. "I'll be trendy."

"Are you sure you want to be trendy?" I asked him. Trib's idea of dressing up was to put on a different cartoon T-shirt, usually featuring some complicated computer-nerd joke.

"For a change." Trib winked. "Anyway, to marry your mom, of course."

"Sounding good," I said. "What about me?"

"Floaty," Mom said, "floaty and coordinated with us, of course."

"Have we got a date on this?" I asked. "Because you might want to fix up the backyard."

"Spring," Mom said, "late spring or early summer. We want to be sure of fine weather. But we'll have a bad-weather contingency plan, of course. A tent or something. We'll set a date, won't we, Trib? Then we can do the invitations."

"We'll do it whenever you like, baby," Trib said.

I raised my eyebrows. I could not get used to the way Trib called Mom baby. She was a self-declared feminist. It was dangerous territory. Or it should have been. Mom just nestled up to him and smiled. "Oh, please," I said, "she's old enough to be my mother!" They ignored me.

Was it going to be like this when Spooky and Dad got together? I'd be surrounded by kissing grown-ups. Gross. This wasn't supposed to happen. By the time kids are my age, adults should be over the kissing-in-public thing. They can do it privately, but publicly it should just be a quick kiss and on with the business, nothing lingering. Now, if it was Richard and me, that would be different. As soon as I started to think about that, my mind shut down like Mom's old laptop used to do when it overheated.

I stayed out of their way for most of the weekend. I wrote the Chronicles.

# Holly and Eclipse

"And now," the Abbot said, patting his mouth with his napkin, "I invite the newly wedded couple to rise from their seats and dance as man and wife."

But before Lady Tamsin and Lord Treece could begin their stately dance, there was a clap of thunder and a light flashed in the feasting hall, blinding everyone except the already-blind harpist.

"Never," shrieked a voice, "they should never dance as man and wife!"

Blinking, Lady Rosa beheld a girl, no older than herself, with dirty brown hair and a slightly grubby face. In one hand she held a staff decorated at the top with a great crystal, and in the other she held a scrawny black cat. She looked somewhat familiar, but Lady Rosa couldn't place her. She turned to see her mother's reaction. Her mother was advancing on the girl, one hand extended graciously to greet the unexpected guest and her best hostess smile on her face.

Polly's hair is sometimes a little dirty—not that Holly is Polly, but I simply had to base my witch on someone;

otherwise how could I write about her? I wasn't sure yet why Rosa thought she was slightly familiar. I just threw that in for a bit of tension to keep the reader interested. The problem with that kind of thing, though, was that you had to remember what you'd thrown in while you wrote the rest of it. Perhaps Holly could be Lord Burgundy's illegitimate daughter with some forest witch. That wasn't a bad thought. I paused to write it down in my notebook and plowed on.

*"I'm afraid we haven't been properly introduced," Lady Tamsin said, delicately clasping the young girl's hand in such as way as to mostly avoid contact with it and definitely avoid being in reach of the cat, which had flattened its ears at her approach and was flexing its paws to show off unnaturally sharp claws.*

*"That's right, we haven't," the girl said, "but I'm Witch Holly, and this is Eclipse."*

Took me ages to come up with the name Eclipse. I tried all sorts of other names first, but they'd all been used before. How many black cats called Midnight does the world need?

*"Welcome, my dear. This is my husband, Lord Treece."*

*Lord Treece stepped forward and bowed low over the girl's hand. He, too, avoided the cat's gaze and withdrew as soon as he could. He sneezed.*

*"Sorry," he said, "allergies. Nothing against Eclipse, just an involuntary reaction."*

Did they know about allergies then? Well, it was a fantasy. I could bend the rules a bit. I liked the idea of Lord Treece sneezing away while Lady Burgundy frowned and the Witch Holly narrowed her eyes.

"Your husband—which husband, Lady Burgundy?"

"My second husband, of course," Lady Burgundy said. There was an edge in her voice that Lady Rosa recognized instantly. It was the same edge that sent her scurrying to her room to finish her lessons. Witch Holly seemed unaware of the danger she could be in.

"My first has been declared dead. He has been neither seen nor heard from for the requisite number of years. I missed him sorely for the first decade, Witch Holly. But enough is enough, I'm sure you'll agree."

"It would be, if your first husband wasn't still alive!" Although the girl scarcely raised her voice, all the wedding guests heard. The Abbot turned pale and poured another glass of wine. Lord Treece looked quickly at his new wife and took her hand in his.

"How do you know?" he asked simply.

"I saw it in my scriving bowl," she answered, "and the Old Ones sent me here to tell you before it was too late. But I couldn't find Eclipse. Looked for him everywhere. Blasted cat was hiding. He hates traveling. So I am too late, aren't I?"

"Not only too late, but your evidence is very slight," Lady Burgundy said smoothly. "I think we shall have to keep you here until new evidence comes to light."

I was proud of the way Lady Burgundy just went on as though her party wasn't ruined by this witch upstart calling her a bigamist in front of everyone.

"You're not putting me in——."

But it was too late. Guards had seized the young witch and grabbed her magic staff before she could use it against them. Without it she was powerless. Eclipse jumped from her arms and disappeared during the shouting and struggle. No one except Lady Rosa saw him go. She wondered if she should run after him and catch him, but she loved animals and couldn't bear the thought of the cat, too, being locked in the dungeon, so she let him go.

If only she hadn't. But she didn't know about witches' cats then.

More tension added. I leaned back in my chair. This was going better than it had for ages. I was on a roll. Thank heavens—I needed one!

The dungeon was dark as night, and the walls were as clammy as perspiring flesh, but cold. Holly shivered.

"They can see in the dark," one of the guards said to the other. "No need to leave a candle."

Poor Holly couldn't. Without her magic staff and cat, she was relatively powerless. She was only an apprentice witch, after all. Scriving and the lesser spells she could do with the appropriate equipment, but she hadn't learned the other magic. The Old Ones had noticed a definite talent in her for scriving, so they'd concentrated on developing that rather than the more useful things like night vision. She huddled in a corner listening to the scrabbles of what she recognized as rats and wished she knew a lot more than she did.

Meanwhile, in another part of the castle, the guests were dancing, but there was a certain awkwardness about the festivities, despite Lady Tamsin's graciousness, the blind harpist's most soothing and jolly tunes, and the quantities of ale and wine being poured.

"I say," Ricardo said in Lady Rosa's ear, "do you think this might be true?"

Her heart was thumping so loudly she thought everyone would be able to hear it. My father, she thought, my father, still alive! But when she answered Ricardo, her tone was as quiet and calm as her mother's had been. "I have no idea," she said. "Really, these people come out of the woods and declare themselves servants of the Old Ones, but half of them are just after money. You know how it is, I'm sure."

Ricardo looked down at her. She was paler than ever, he thought, but the slight smile that met his look betrayed nothing of her thoughts. She would make a wonderful wife, he thought— beautiful and clever. What more could a man want?

"Shall we step outside?" he asked. "The moonlight makes the parapet an inviting place to dally."

Lady Rosa swallowed. No man before had asked her such a thing. But it was a good time for it, while her mother's attention was diverted. It was really now or never. She bent her head, and they walked slowly toward the great doors that opened onto the parapet.

Actually, I wasn't sure what a parapet was. I googled it, and it turned out it was a narrow walkway around a wall. Perhaps a garden would have been a better place for them to make out? But I liked the sound of the parapet. Also, they could lean on the wall and see the castle grounds stretch out in front of them. The moon would shine on them. No, the moon would *beam* on them while they kissed.

But how did I write about kissing? What would Lady Rosa feel? I'd never kissed anyone—not like that.

I tried it on my hand. It just felt strangely as though I was sort of munching my own hand. Yuck. I could probably have gone into the living room and spied on some kissing. Trib and Mom were watching some romantic war movie in there. But I could hardly go in there with my notebook and take notes.

There's always some hitch with writing. Like in the e-mails from Dad, when I'd just think, yes, I've got it right, and I'd sail along confidently saying this and that. Then I'd realize Spooky had asked me an unanswerable question, like "Where do you see yourself in five years' time, Max?" What kind of question was that, anyway?

Why did they have to kiss? Would Lady Rosa enjoy it? Would I enjoy it?

*"You are very beautiful," Ricardo said as they surveyed the view before them. It was a full moon, and the grounds were lit up as though specially for them. Farther away, the forest was a shadowy mass of trees.*

*"Thank you." Lady Rosa's heart was beating wildly. She thought he might kiss her. The setting was right; the mood was right. Would he?*

*As though he knew what she was thinking, he took one of her hands and raised it to his mouth, looking at her the entire time. His mouth lingered on her hand. She didn't try to pull her hand away.*

I left them there, because Dad had driven into Mom's driveway and was tooting the horn.

I'd decided to warm him up to the idea of meeting Spooky. I'd worked out my plan and put it into action practically as soon as I was in the car.

"I'm sick of being an only child," I told him. "It's boring. There's never anyone to play with. Like this weekend—Mom and Trib did nothing but discuss wedding stuff. Boring."

"Well, I can't do anything about that," Dad said, "and neither can your mom, I wouldn't think. She wouldn't want to start a new family at her age. Babies and toddlers are hard work, and kids are just plain expensive."

"But you could meet someone who already had a kid," I pointed out. "That would be ideal. I'd have a stepbrother."

"I'm not rushing into a new relationship just to satisfy your demands, kiddo," Dad said, "and anyway, it wouldn't necessarily be a stepbrother. I might meet someone with a girl. How would you feel then? Not the only princess around the place!"

I chose to ignore this remark.

"I think you should start going out with people again," I said. "It's not good being by yourself all the time."

"Is this another one of your campaigns?" Dad sounded a bit cranky.

"Not a campaign, exactly," I said, "just an opinion. There was an article in today's paper about Internet dating."

Dad snorted. "I don't think so, Magenta. Really!"

"Don't be such an old stick-in-the-mud. Everyone's doing it. People are meeting really wonderful people online. They're getting married and everything."

"Call me old-fashioned, but I like meeting someone face-to-face and feeling whether the chemistry's right."

"Well, that's tough," I said, "because where are you going to meet this chemistry experiment if you never go out?"

"All in good time," Dad said, reaching over to pat my knee, "all in good time, Magenta."

"It's not looking good," I whispered to Polly later on the phone. "He wants chemistry, not e-mails."

"He can't get chemistry until he meets her," Polly said practically. "You'll have to talk him into it. I'm sure when he hears the whole story, he'll be game."

I wasn't. Polly hadn't experienced Dad's stubbornness firsthand, the way I had. But she was right—I would have to talk him into it and sooner than we thought, because when I checked, there was an e-mail from Spooky suggesting they meet for coffee. She talked about chemistry, too. Why did adults harp on chemistry? I decided it could all wait until the next day. I was too stressed to deal with it. What with the kissing in the Chronicles, Trib and Mom's wedding, and Dad's refusal to even read the newspaper article on Internet dating, I was almost looking forward to school.

# Spells and Sausages

I'd completely forgotten that it was the all-school run the next day. Fortunately Mom called me first thing to remind me to wear lots of blue for my team, Blue Team (why couldn't they come up with better team names—Dragon Team, for example, Tiger Team, Team of Happiness—but no, we get boring old colors). Then Polly called while Dad was trying to put my hair into lots of little braids so I could use all the blue ribbon we'd found from last year.

"Look out the window," she said in a mysterious voice.

Dad and I shuffled to the window and looked out.

"So?"

"The weather prediction today was for sun. Nothing but sun. See those gray clouds?"

I looked up at the sky. There were more clouds than blue patches. "Yeah?"

"My work. That's all I'll say. Oh, and bring a raincoat. Over and out."

"What was that all about?"

"Polly hates running," I told him, "so she's hoping for rain."

"Well, it certainly looks as though you'll get a few drops," Dad said. "Good for our veggies."

"Wouldn't you like to meet someone who loved veggies as much as you do? You could both do the weeding together." I knew how corny it sounded. I just wanted him to think about it while I huffed and puffed through the race. Actually, I like this kind of running—I don't care about winning; I just like the whole running-along-the-path thing. You see little wrens and butterflies, and it's a change from school.

"I'm happy; thanks, Magenta. Hey, I'll drive you to school today. I'm helping with the library Book Sale and Sausage Sizzle. So when you finish school, you can come up to the library. I'll probably still be there."

"The library's having a Sausage Sizzle?"

"My idea." Dad looked pleased. "Something different. Libraries need to lift their community profile. Get a bit more with the action. Offer something relevant."

"Sausages?"

"Fund-raising."

"Well, that's good, Dad. I mean, it's terrific that you're involved." I was delighted. It would be another topic of conversation with old Spooky. She'd be just the kind of person who would find that awesome, not lame.

It started to rain almost as soon as we got in the car.

"Good thing the Sizzle's under shelter," Dad said, checking out the gray clouds, "and it might clear up, too— look at the horizon. What time is your race?"

"About ten, I think. The buses leave school almost as soon as we get there."

"Well, good luck, break a leg—not!" Dad kissed me good-bye. He was almost too cheerful.

Polly was happy, too. She kept looking at the sky and counting the gray clouds. She was wearing a raincoat, even though it was just misting. "Look at that," she hissed at me. "Just look at it!"

"Clouds, Polly, just clouds."

"My clouds," Polly said, "that's the difference. I conjured these up with a spell."

"You what?"

She nodded. "I'm getting better, aren't I?" She said it so smugly I wanted the sun to break through the clouds and shine right into her eyes. But it didn't. Instead the rain got a bit heavier, and everyone in the bus line started to complain.

"We're not going to have to run in this?"

"My sneakers will get soaked, and Mom'll kill me."

"So? Mine are suede."

"Ms. Olley, we don't have to run if it rains, do we?"

"Call this rain?" Ms. Olley smiled in a way that meant she wasn't at all amused. "This is just a mere sprinkle. Children these days. Wimps."

It rained the entire bus trip. It rained as the teachers put up the first-aid tent. The Red Team crepe ribbons ran in the rain and left streaks of pink across faces, arms, and white T-shirts. They ran all the way down Ms. Mann's lace blouse. She kept looking down at the drips and trying to rub them off.

"I can't run in the rain." Polly approached Ms. Mann. "I'm getting a cold, and Jane expressly said that if it even looked like rain, I should just sit in the first-aid tent. She would have kept me home, but she's doing cupcakes today for some celebrity thing, and Marcus was busy finding his muse."

"I'm afraid"—Ms. Mann glared down at another pink drop and at Polly—"that the first-aid tent is usually too full by the end of this run for us to take in spectators. Anyway, I believe the rain's clearing—look!"

Sure enough, the blue patches now outnumbered the gray clouds, and they seemed to be skittering away behind us. Polly frowned, and I could see her lips move frantically.

"Get in line, then." Ms. Mann fluttered her hands at us. "Quickly."

Almost as soon as the starting signal rang, the sun came out, as though it was blessing our run. The rain made the air smell like lemon and eucalyptus and wet sand. Polly settled into a grumpy walk, but I stretched out my legs and ran for a while. The sandy path was good to run on—not as springy as grass but not thuddy like the pavement. I kept running—even when my legs felt wobbly. I ran through that feeling and found my rhythm again. I didn't care about winning. I was just enjoying it—it felt as though someone had let me loose after days of sitting at a desk.

"Well done, Magenta McPhee!" Mr. Green gave me a green ribbon. "This must be a personal best for you. Third place!"

Blue Team kids I hardly knew slapped my back. I

couldn't believe it—third place! I didn't think of myself as being one of the sports jocks. Well, I wasn't. I was a fantasy writer. But maybe I could run, too. It felt good.

About ten minutes later Polly shuffled bad-temperedly past the finish line. She was blowing her nose repeatedly and loudly into a clean tissue.

"Jane will kill me." She glared at everyone. "I'm not allowed to get a cold. Marcus has his exhibition opening this weekend, and they're counting on me to be on deck to mind the brat, I mean Jeremy. She'll kill me." And she blew her nose again. You could tell she was faking.

"I came in third." I waved my ribbon at her. "Third place, Polly!"

"Good for you," she said sourly. "Next it'll be the marathon."

"Well, hardly," I said, falling into step with her as we headed to the barbecue, where Mr. Tanner was dispensing sausages and burgers. "But I might do some training. See if I can get second next year. I mean, it's good for a fantasy writer to do something physical as well. It can help you write. I read that somewhere."

"I'm a vegetarian," Polly told Mr. Tanner. "I did inform the school of this at the beginning of the year, and I was told that my needs would be catered to."

"Have a sausage, then," Mr. Tanner said. "I wouldn't guarantee there was any meat in these."

"The preservatives in sausages don't agree with me," Polly said. "I would have thought it was easy enough for the school to arrange for some marinated tofu for the vegetarians. I can't be the only one."

"The others provide their own lunch," Mr. Tanner pointed out. Most teachers would have already yelled at Polly by now, but Mr. Tanner was only six months away from retirement and was determinedly cheerful under all circumstances. We knew this because he'd told us. Which was a mistake, really, because at first everyone had wanted to make him yell. We gave up, though. His patience was simply greater than ours.

"My mother is doing cupcakes for seventy today," Polly said. Her grumpiness had gone, and she was just enjoying jousting with a teacher. "She didn't have time to prepare a special lunch for me as well. Marcus, who is, as you probably know, a reasonably prominent sculptor, is looking for his muse. His exhibition opens this weekend, and he's worried that he'll get artist's block immediately after the opening and have to lie in a darkened room for a week like last time. So there was no one to make me lunch this morning, Mr. Tanner."

Mr. Tanner flipped a burger onto a waiting bun, topped it with fried onion, squeezed a dollop of sauce over it, and handed it to me. "Congratulations, Magenta McPhee," he said. "Third prize for Blue Team—that'll boost our results, won't it? Come back if you want a sausage." And he winked at me before turning back to Polly. "I wasn't suggesting that your parents should prepare you alternatives to our traditional post-race fare, but rather that you were old enough yourself to anticipate hunger in the face of our carnivorous repast."

I wished I had my notebook with me. Listening to

Mr. Tanner was like reading a fantasy novel. I should have been taking notes. Mind you, he only talked this way with Polly. Otherwise he was pretty normal.

"Our fridge is full of cupcake mix," Polly said, "and wax castings, Jane's white wine, and the brat's antibiotics. He has a middle-ear infection but went to day care anyway this morning because he could actually stand up without falling over. I'm practically an abandoned child, Mr. Tanner."

"Then have a sausage, Polly." Mr. Tanner smiled at her. "Abandoned children sometimes must abandon their principles in order to survive."

Polly sighed. "I'll have barbecue sauce, not ketchup, thanks," she said.

I pinned my green ribbon to my shorts. Everyone could see it and would know I'd gotten third place.

"So," Polly said, "well done, Magenta. I guess I could help you train. You'll need a motivator."

The sausage had cured her bad temper.

"That could be good," I said. "Like a personal trainer?"

"More than that," Polly said. "A motivator is with you every step of the way. It's a new thing. I read about it online. Did you see my rain? All I needed to do was spend a bit more time on that spell, and I'd have it perfected. It was great, wasn't it? Nothing in the forecast about rain today—that was all mine."

"You are getting better." I squeezed her arm. "Good job, Polly! You have the third-prize rainmaking ribbon—a new category in the race!"

"Thanks." Polly grinned at me. "Wait until I can make love potions. Who do you like? I've got my eyes on Adam Lister."

"Adam Lister!"

"Why not?" Polly stuck her chin out. "He's only two grades ahead."

"But he's hot, Polly. He's hot and he's with Katey, and they've been together, like, for ages."

"I'll wait until he's free," Polly conceded. "I think it's unethical to break people up—it's against my feminist principles. Sisterhood is sacred. I'll practice on Hentley, I think."

Hentley was a year above us. He wasn't exactly hot, but he had a good smile, great ears, and he clowned around as though everything was okay in his world, when we all knew that his dad had walked out, leaving his mom with three kids and no job. Hentley couldn't afford to buy school textbooks but borrowed them from the library. He worked on weekends, mowing lawns and stuff, and gave the money to his mom. Hentley was cool in an uncool way.

"I don't think you should practice on anyone," I said. "What happens if Hentley falls head over heels and you're just toying with his emotions? That's not very ethical, Polly."

"I might fall head over heels, too," Polly said calmly. "I like Hentley. He has values."

There were times when Polly sounded as though she was someone's mother. I put it down to her being the daughter of Jane and Marcus, who talked about everything in front of her.

"What about you?" she turned to me. "Who shall you use my love potion on?"

I shook my head. I wasn't going to play.

"Not still pining after Richard?"

I shrugged.

"Magenta! It's been years."

"Three years, two months, three weeks, and one day," I said. I kept a record.

Polly shook her head. "That's crazy, Mags. You should get out more, live a little. You are too much your father's daughter."

"Well, that's not true," I said. "I have to be my father's daughter, because I am. Anyway, constancy is a good thing. Everyone in fantasy books is as constant as the day."

"Yes, but we aren't living in fantasy, Mags. We're in the contemporary world, and it's standard practice now for girls to have crushes on many, many boys, right through high school and college. We should probably all go out with at least ten different guys before we graduate. Then, eventually, when the biological clock's winding down a little, we find the One and marry him. After eleven-point-five years, we divorce him and find another Mr. Right. That's the modern way."

"Jane and Marcus aren't divorced."

"Marcus is too used to Jane's cooking," Polly said. "He'd never leave Jane. Jane's got this thing about happy families. She'd do anything to keep it together. And she does work at it—always pestering Marcus to do meditation classes with her and couples' massage. Marcus goes along with it, but you can tell he's just zoning out."

"I don't care," I said, trying to fray the bottom of my third-place ribbon. "I can't help who I am."

Polly looked at me seriously and nodded. "No," she said, "you can't. That's true."

When I got home from school, Dad was sitting in the living room with curtains drawn, listening to some mournful music.

"I got third place!" I said, waving my ribbon at him. "In the all-school run."

"Well done, Magenta!" he said. "Let me see."

I turned on the light so he could admire the ribbon. "What's wrong?"

"Nothing," he said, stretching his mouth into a smile, "nothing at all. I've just been sitting here listening. You can hear better in the dark, you know."

"How was the Sausage Sizzle?"

"The usual—the sausages sizzled. People bought them. Good thing, really, that the rain didn't last all that long. It might have deterred people from coming out. We—the library—made quite a bit of money. I was personally thanked for my part in making it happen."

"So why are you sitting in the dark, looking unhappy?"

"I'm not—well, I'm not deliberately looking unhappy. I was just listening to some music."

"Mournful music," I said, "as if you wanted the music to cry along with you."

"Don't be ridiculous, Magenta. Come on, now, how will we celebrate this wonderful ribbon?"

We ended up ordering pizza for dinner and renting a DVD. I'd chosen, so it was a love story. I wanted to get Dad in the mood for my news. I'd decided that the best thing I could do was simply tell him the truth. It was because of something that Mr. Tanner had mentioned earlier in the day while comforting Josh Lynam, who'd twisted his ankle on the last bend and missed first place for the first time in three years.

"You did your best, Josh," he'd said, popping two sausages in the bun. "That's all you can do in this world. You did your best, but the fates were against you on that last bend. Could have happened to anyone. You just tell your dad that you did your best and that's what counts. Heavens, I saw you pick yourself up and limp on—not all kids would have bothered. You're a trooper, Josh."

I know that didn't sound as though it was a very inspirational message for me. I mean, my ankles were fine, and I wasn't worried about running, anyway. But what I thought when I heard Mr. Tanner say it was how I'd only done my best in the whole Spooky thing, and what was the worst thing that could happen when I told Dad? He wasn't going to kick me out of the house. He wasn't going to hit me—like we all thought Josh's dad might do, though no one knew for sure. He might yell for a while, or do that sighing, I'm-so-disappointed thing they do. But I'd still be alive at the end of the night, and so would he. He'd come in, like he always did, to wish me good night, kiss me on the forehead, and stroke my hair off my face. I might be grounded for a week, but so what? Things wouldn't change all that much.

I sat down at the computer and printed out all the e-mails between Dad and Spooky. I printed out the profile Polly and I had written for him, and Spooky's profile, too. I took them into the living room. Dad had put on more music, but it was a little happier this time.

"Hey, there, marathon girl," he said, "what's up?"

"I've got something to tell you," I said, "or show you, really."

I handed him the stack of paper and sat down on the sofa, waiting.

"What is all this?" Dad asked. "Why is my photo on this?"

"Just read it, please, Dad. And remember, I only did it to make you happy."

There was silence while Dad read the first couple of pages. I picked at the skin around my fingernails. I really wanted long nails I could paint with glittery colors, but I always picked at them when I was anxious, so it never happened. I tried to think what colors I'd like my nails to be. I imagined purple and orange. Then I looked at Dad. He was frowning. I stopped trying to think of other things and just wondered what he was going to say to me—and how I was going to persuade him to still meet Spooky.

"Oh, Magenta," Dad said when he was about six pages in, "why on earth did you think this was a good idea?"

"You aren't meeting anyone," I said. "Mom's getting married, and you're still drooping around. Everyone's Internet-dating these days—even Polly's grandmother."

"I should have known Polly was in on this! How long has this been going on?"

"A few weeks. It's been harder and harder to write the e-mails."

"I'm surprised you managed at all," Dad said. He came over to where I sat and ruffled my hair. "I guess this is just another facet of your writing career?"

"So you're not angry?"

"Well, I'm not happy. I think this probably counts as identity fraud and could be punished by law. But I'm mainly sad that you've been thinking I'm so sad. There have been a few setbacks, I admit. Today I was feeling sad because . . . well, never mind. Generally speaking, though, I'm okay, Magenta. It's hard when everything you thought was working goes bottom up, but it's a good time to reassess, and that's what I've been doing."

I didn't want to hear the reassessment speech—I'd heard it too many times before. "But you will meet her," I interrupted him. "You'll have coffee with Spoo . . . I mean Lianna?"

"I most certainly will not!" Dad said. "You'll e-mail this poor woman and tell her the truth immediately, Magenta."

"But Dad, why? Why won't you just have coffee with her? What harm would that do?"

"It puts us both in a false position," Dad said. "She'll think I'm interested in her and I'm not, and I'll know that this was your doing. No, Magenta."

"How do you know you're not interested in her?" I said desperately. "She's really quite pretty in an old kind of way."

Dad looked at the photo I'd printed out in color. "Yes, she is," he conceded. "She has warm eyes."

"So if you met her at a party or—a Sausage Sizzle, you might ask her to coffee."

Dad looked at me oddly and frowned. "What do you mean, if I met her at a Sausage Sizzle?" he asked sharply.

"Nothing." I didn't understand. Why was he giving me the Look? Dad glared at me for a few seconds and then went back to studying the photo.

"I might," he said slowly, "but it would depend on the chemistry between us. When a man and a woman meet, there's a certain chemistry, and I've always trusted that. Your mom and I had it. I had it with—well, a couple of people."

"But Dad," I plowed on, "how would you know if you had it with Spooky if you didn't meet her? You might completely waste this opportunity, and the chemistry might have zinged between you. She's got a son, you know. Have you read that far?"

"I'll read them all," Dad said, "while you go and do your homework. Then we'll talk about it."

I sat in my room staring at the English questions in our workbook. It seemed to take Dad ages to read through the e-mails, though he sprinted through his library books. When he finally came into my room, it was past my bedtime and I was yawning.

"This was just not a good thing to do," he said, putting the e-mails in a heap on my desk. "But I do understand that you were worried, and I admire both you and Polly for your writing skills. You've put me in a very difficult position, Magenta. I think this woman is genuinely looking for someone to share her life with—"

"And you're not? You want to grow old all by yourself beside a pile of library books?"

"That's enough, Magenta. As I was saying, you've put this woman and me in a very awkward position. I think we have to meet her—if only to apologize. You will come along with me, and you'll tell her the whole truth. I think we owe her that much. She's put a lot of effort into this communication."

"So have I!"

"That's rather the point," Dad said grimly. "I haven't, but she thinks I have, and she's told you—not me—intimate details of her life. We owe her a big apology."

In the end Dad e-mailed Spooky a longish e-mail, saying that he'd like to meet her for coffee, but he'd be bringing me along to clear up certain issues. I thought it sounded ominous, but Dad said that it was an adult thing and probably Spooky would guess before she even met us for coffee, and that would lessen the blow.

"You might like her," I pointed out sleepily.

"I might. But I doubt it—I mean, I'm sure she's a very nice person, but I wouldn't get your hopes up, Magenta. She sounds a little—"

"She's just lonely," I said, "that's all. Anyone can be lonely."

"That's true," Dad said, "but I've got you, Magenta." He kissed me good night, and I wondered briefly why he sounded sad when he said that, but I was too tired to give it any proper thought.

# Five-Star Expectations

Dad was on the computer checking his e-mail when I got up the next morning.

"She must be interested," he said. "Look, Mags, she replied within ten minutes of my sending my e-mail. She must have been sitting at her computer."

"She could've just been googling stuff," I said. "It doesn't mean she was waiting for you to reply." But I didn't say it with much conviction. In my experience, Spooky replied with unexpected speed.

"Poor woman," Dad said. "Listen, she's going to bring along her son, too—Cal, she's bringing Cal. Well, that will be good—it means she's not expecting any romance."

"How could she when you said you'd bring me along?"

"That's true—still, it's gracious of her to reciprocate by bringing along her child. I think that's quite brave of her."

"Are we still going to tell her it was me that set up your profile and wrote the e-mails?" I felt Dad's attitude toward the whole thing was softening.

"We certainly are, Magenta."

Apparently his position hadn't weakened enough.

"So when do we meet them?"

"She's suggested midweek, after school. She lives only two suburbs away. That's interesting. Perhaps we should go to that organic place? The one with the great chocolate muffins. I bet Cal eats chocolate muffins."

"Sure," I said. I wasn't worried about Cal; I liked chocolate muffins.

"So, I'll e-mail her back later and arrange it all," Dad said. "Now, don't you have school today?"

I was already halfway out of the room—I wanted to get to school to tell Polly the latest update. This was getting exciting.

"So he's agreed to see her?" Polly said, balancing her books in a precarious pile under one arm as she rummaged around in her locker for her pencil case. "That's got to be a good start. And you weren't grounded."

"But I have to explain it all to her," I pointed out. "That's not so great. And her son will be there—which will make it twice as embarrassing."

"He might be very cool," Polly said. "Though it's probably against the rules for step-siblings to fall in love."

"Don't be stupid, Polly. It's coffee."

"Everything starts with coffee." Polly raised her eyebrows. "Don't you know that yet, Magenta McPhee?"

When I got home from school, Dad was still on the computer. It was such an unusual sight that I misjudged throwing my school bag on the couch, and it landed on the glass-topped coffee table with a crash.

"Do be more careful, Magenta," Dad said without looking up.

"What are you doing?"

He turned around then, looking a bit sheepish. "Oh, just, you know, talking to Lianna."

"On MSN?"

"Yes. Is there anything wrong with that?"

"No, of course not, but I didn't think you were interested—"

"She was asking my advice about Cal," Dad said, sounding a little defensive. "She's worried about the lack of male role models in his life. She's worried that he's too protective of her. Well, I know what that feels like!"

"I'm not protective!" I protested. "I just want you to have a life."

"Whereas Cal gets worried when Lianna has a life," Dad said. "Same problem, different outcome."

"I'm just glad you're all getting along so well," I said. "And now I have homework to do, so don't let me disturb you, Dr. Max."

"Who's huffy?" Dad laughed.

"Not me. I've just got things to do."

Without the added hassle of inventing Dad's e-mails, I sped through my homework and had time to work on the Chronicles. I decided that the whole kissing question could be left on the parapet and I should concentrate on Holly instead. I did the three-stars thing writers do when they want to change scenes without starting a new chapter.

In her corner, Holly waited for something to happen. The worst thing about the dungeon, apart from the dark and the rats, was the boredom. She tried to remember all the spells she'd ever been taught and managed to make a little dancing light that she couldn't keep still. It spun around the dungeon, lighting up the piles of rubble on the floor, the scratch marks on the stone walls that she imagined had been made by past prisoners, and the odd tail flick of a scared rat. The dungeon was just as bad seen in the light as it had felt in the dark, but the light was comforting, and Holly felt less helpless, because she had made it happen.

I sat up straighter. That was how I should feel about Dad and Spooky. Sure, I had to explain to her that I was responsible for Dad's early e-mails, but in the end, he was talking to her on MSN. I'd made that happen. The idea of meeting Spooky seemed less daunting.

Holly started to follow the light around the cell, looking for a way out. There wasn't one. The door was thick wood with great iron bars running both ways. The one little window was bolted shut from the other side and set flush against the door—letting not even the thinnest streak of light in from the outside. It wasn't until Holly's little light danced on the roof of the cell that she saw another window, high up in the wall. Although it was barred, there was no wooden shutter—it was open, though to what, Holly had no idea. She guessed, from the fact that no light shone through it, that it was just open to the next cell. It was far too high for her to investigate, but it was there—that was something. Just as the light danced away to another place, there was a meow from the window, and she caught the green light of a cat's eyes.

"Eclipse?" she whispered.

"Meow."

"Oh, Eclipse, can you jump?"

"Meow."

"But perhaps you'd better not. You'd never get back up there from down here, and you're better off being outside than trapped in here with me, much as I'd like company."

"Meow."

I stopped writing. I wasn't sure about adding all Eclipse's meows. To me, when I said them aloud, they all sounded different, but would a reader be able to grasp that? I doubted it. If I read woofs, for example, in a book, they'd all just sound like woofs. I'd have to send Eclipse away or give him the power of speech. I didn't want to do that. A bit of telepathy, maybe, but no speech. I hated books with talking animals. That was just cheating. Fortunately it was bedtime, so I could stop. As I brushed my teeth, I wondered how adult writers managed, who had no bedtime or even homework to do. Did they just work on and on until they were so tired they had to stop? Or did they invent things that had to be done when they couldn't write any more?

I decided that when I was a grown-up writer, I'd have a whole list of things I had to do. That way I could stop writing whenever I felt like it. I'd copy the list Mom kept on her cell phone: *Pay bills, Do laundry, Cook ahead, Meeting preparation!* But I'd add some good things, too: *Go to beach, See movie, Play Flight of the Hamsters!*

Dad said he'd pick me up at school on Wednesday, and that way we'd arrive at the Go Green Café about the same time as Cal and Spooky, who I had to remember to call Lianna.

"But then I'll still be in school uniform."

"So?"

"Dad, it's sooo tacky. No one gets seen anywhere in uniform if they can help it."

I'd had my outfit planned. I was going to wear my black jeans and the purple velvet top Dad had gotten for me at the consignment shop. It was a little bit Goth, but not so Goth that it looked as though I needed to be completely pale and wearing too much black eye makeup, particularly if I wore my patterned sneakers. It would be an outfit entirely suited to someone who was writing her first fantasy novel and who might be excused for worrying about her dad so much that she put his profile up on an Internet dating site without his permission. Also there was Cal. He might just turn out to be . . . well, not like Richard, of course, but having potential.

"You're not being seen anywhere," Dad said. "We're just all having coffee at the Go Green."

"I just thought I'd wear something good. Can't we whiz home first? Just so I can change quickly? I'd only be a minute."

"Magenta, I'm not going to be late, okay? Being on time is a matter of courtesy. In this case, particularly, I think the least we owe Lianna and her son is a little courtesy. Don't forget why we're meeting them."

"Okay." I sighed heavily. I cheered myself up by wearing my favorite lip gloss—Pinkly Bare—and putting the tiniest bit of mascara on my eyelashes. Actually, it wasn't my mascara but a tube I'd borrowed from Mom, so it was a bit sticky, and I ended up with drops of it stuck to the ends of my lashes and I had to scrub most of it off with a washcloth.

"You look tired," Polly said the minute she saw me. "Were you up late planning what to say on the Big Day?"

"No," I said.

"You've got dark circles under your eyes," she said. "Maybe you've just inherited them from your dad. I'm going to go gray early, according to Jane. But you can always use dye to fix that. You'd better put some concealer on before you meet Spooky's son."

"I haven't got any concealer," I said. "It can't be that bad; Dad didn't say anything."

When we went into the girls' bathroom, though, I could see what Polly meant. The skin underneath my eyes— the left in particular—was kind of dark. I dabbed Polly's cover-up stick at the shadows.

"I didn't know you used this stuff," I said, examining it.

"I don't," Polly said darkly. "It's Jane's. She makes me carry around spare stuff in case she forgets. It was after the enormous hormonal-pimple episode. She had to meet a client. You can imagine the rest. I'm telling you, that woman has already cost me years of income in future therapy."

"What do I do now? It looks as though I've got some skin condition just underneath my eyes."

"You dab it with a wet washcloth. We'll have to use toilet paper. That kind of smooths it into your skin."

When we dabbed, some of the dark shadows came off with the Peachy Beige concealer.

"Mascara," I said, examining the toilet paper. "That's a relief. I'd hate to end up looking like Dad."

"Maybe you'll just go gray early too," Polly said, flushing away the evidence. "So you've prepared your speech? Or just your makeup? Which I assume is for the boy's benefit?"

"I'm going to wing it." I ignored Polly's last remark. "I think it will sound better if it's more natural."

"The spontaneous effect," Polly said, nodding. "Probably a good idea. Still, if I were you, I would have made some notes at least. After all, they'll all be listening."

She meant the boy. I knew that. But Cal meant nothing to me. Richard was the man I loved. Unless, of course, Cal turned out to be practice-worthy like Hentley, but without Hentley's added issues that made it mean to even think of practicing on him. Though Cal already had Spooky, who was probably an issue all by herself.

When I tried to tell Polly all this, she stuck her fingers in her ears. "Enough with Richard," she said, shutting her eyes so tightly that they turned into little crease marks on her face. "Enough already. He's never going to look at you. Not until you're seventeen at least. It's doomed, Mags, really doomed. He's practically a man—though Jane figures men are boys until forty, which makes Marcus barely an adolescent. But if you take away the Jane factor, Richard is almost a man. Not only that, but he's practically a cousin. That's illegal."

"Richard's a *step*-first cousin, not a real anything, because he's Trib's nephew. So there, Polly Davies."

"It would still be wrong. Unless you met in some romantic city, like Paris, say, when you were a young woman and he didn't even recognize you but invited you out anyway, even though you were with some dude."

"As if, Polly."

"Well, that's what I mean, Magenta. You've got to give him up. Set your sights on someone less out of your reach."

"Like Hentley?" I hadn't meant to say that. It slipped out because I'd been thinking of him just before. To my surprise, Polly went red. Not pink, but red. As though she'd been running, which Polly never does.

"Not Hentley precisely," she said, "but, yeah, that kind of thing."

"We don't even know what Cal looks like," I protested. "He could be like the Missing Link, for all we know. At least Richard's gorgeous."

"Cal might be even hotter," Polly pointed out.

"I suppose," I said, but I knew he couldn't be better-looking than Richard.

He wasn't. We walked into the Go Green at precisely 3:25 p.m., and Spooky—sorry, Lianna—and Cal were already sitting at a table. She was sitting facing the door, not even pretending to read the open newspaper in front of her. He was sitting to her left, bent over a handheld PlayStation.

She looked almost exactly like her photo, just a couple of years older, and the blond streaks in her hair were growing out, so you could see the dark roots. I wondered if she'd recently waxed the hairs above her top lip, too, because it looked slightly pink, the way Mom's goes when she's just waxed. Not that Mom ever does that when it matters. She always waits until Trib's away and there's no school. Maybe Spooky didn't know that kind of stuff but was making an effort for her first date. Though it wasn't really a date.

By the time I'd thought all that, she'd done a little kind of sitting-down jump and started to wave at us, then clasped her hands together, still smiling eagerly in our direction.

"Max!" she called, as though we hadn't all seen each other.

"Hi, Lianna." Dad strode to the table and held out his hand to shake hers. She gave him her hand almost as though she expected him to kiss it. Then they introduced Cal and me to each other, and Dad and I sat down. I buried my face in the menu, and I only looked up when Dad said, "So, we have something to confess, don't we, Magenta?" and gave me a bit of shove with his elbow.

I lowered the menu. "It was me," I said. "The whole idea was mine. I even wrote the e-mails. But only because I wanted Dad to meet someone. You sounded really nice, and I thought you both might get along. I didn't want to mislead you. I just wanted Dad to be happy."

Spooky looked confused, so I started again, and even Cal put down his PS to listen. By the third time, it was all clear, and Spooky had grabbed my hand and told me what a wonderful daughter I was, Cal was nodding, and even Dad was harrumphing in a way that meant he wasn't going to admit it but he was proud of me.

"You wrote all those e-mails yourself?" Spooky said. "I'm amazed. Cal, you'd better pay more attention in English—they were really mature."

"That's not English, Mom," Cal said. "In English, all we get to do is answer these dumb questions. We don't get to pretend to be someone else. That's more like drama."

"Well, she certainly has a flair for whatever it is. You must be so proud, Max!"

"Just embarrassed, really," Dad said. "Though your graciousness is heartwarming, Lianna."

"It's just so wonderful witnessing a strong father-and-daughter bond," Lianna said, patting my father's hand. "You have no idea how many dysfunctional single-parent families are out there. But here you two are, really trying to help each other."

Her eyes looked suspiciously moist, but before she had a chance to cry, our coffees and hot chocolates arrived with the famous chocolate muffins.

"It doesn't mean that we can't all be friends," Spooky said, stirring sugar into her coffee and making little patterns in the cappuccino foam. "I do understand, Max, that this puts you in an awkward position, but friendship?" Her voice tilted up at the end of this sentence hopefully and seemed to hang in the air for a second too long.

"Of course," my father said heartily. "We all need

friends! Particularly single parents. The number of times I've wished I could call someone to help with some problem I've had with Magenta!"

"Or just to eat pizza with in front of the television!" Spooky said, still stirring her coffee.

"Or to go for a Sunday stroll after the changeover shift," Dad said. "You know, when you get home and the house seems too quiet."

"That doesn't happen regularly with us," Spooky admitted, "because Cal's dad lives in Queensland now, but Cal goes there for holidays, don't you, darling? So I know what you mean."

Cal had gone back to his game, but he was also listening, unusual for a boy. He nodded at the mention of his name, and his thick fringe of dark hair kind of bounced once. I wished that he would look up again, because I'd been so preoccupied with my confession that I hadn't taken in any of his features. Spooky seemed to read my mind.

"Do put that thing away, Cal," she said. My mother would have sounded grumpy, but Spooky sounded as though she was asking for a favor rather than being stern. "I want us all to get to know each other, and that includes you, Cal. Max and Magenta do lots of great things together. Cal and I"—she turned to me and Dad—"feel that we've gotten a bit stuck in a rut, you know. It seems like there's never quite enough money to do what we'd really like to do. . . . Not that I'm complaining. I know there are people worse off than us. But still. We'd thought of going to Tasmania. Just by ourselves. A kind of chill-out time. I checked the Internet, but everything was just a little expensive. Except if you camped. I don't feel confident about camping, really. It was something Cal's dad and I were always going to do when Cal got a bit older. By the time that happened, we'd split up."

"Camping's pretty easy," I said, "isn't it, Dad? We do it all through the summer holidays. It's not a big deal. You just need good equipment."

"It's all in the equipment," Dad said. "Luckily, we have good stuff. It's no fun camping with holey tents or a faulty stove. I used to do that when I was younger, of course, and didn't even notice. But kids these days—raised with five-star expectations!"

"I know what you mean." Spooky shot Cal a look.

He stared back at her, the corners of his mouth twitching slightly into the smallest of smiles. He had a thin face, like Spooky's, but his eyes were long and darkly fringed. Why do boys always have good eyelashes? His mouth curled up at the edges as though he spent a lot of time doing his little twitchy smile. He didn't look like a five-star kid. He looked like the kind of boy who'd try to be cheerful under most circumstances. I thought Spooky was being mean. Dad must have agreed with me.

"I bet you're more of a stars-for-your-roof than spa-in-your-room kind of guy," Dad said. I hadn't heard him this cheerful for ages. My spirits lifted. Maybe he would fall in love with Spooky after all. Maybe he already had.

"I'm adaptable," Cal said. He gave me a sideways look, sort of as though he was checking me out, but not so obviously that I'd be offended. "I think that's the saving grace of humanity, our adaptability. Don't you, sir?"

"You don't need to call me sir," Dad said, raising his eyebrows. "Max is fine. And yes, I agree with you. Particularly in a world that's changing so rapidly. Adaptability might save us."

"Dad thinks the world is doomed," I told Cal just so he'd look at me properly. He had a high forehead. I'd read somewhere this was a mark of intelligence. "But he also thinks we need to keep doing our little bit. That's why we grow our own veggies and I walk to school, mostly, and we don't have any electrical equipment at all—not even a PlayStation 1."

"My dad gave me this," Cal told me, "to keep me quiet last Christmas. It's more out of guilt than goodness."

"Oh, Cal, I'm sure he thought it would make you happy," Spooky said anxiously. "It does, doesn't it, darling?"

Cal ignored her. "You can have a try if you want," he said, and handed it over to me.

"I'm not very good at these," I said apologetically, "never having had the experience." I glared at Dad, who was too busy doing his global-warming rant at Spooky to take any notice.

"Here, it's easy—you just shoot at those little dudes when they poke their heads up. See?"

I tried, but they kept coming at me too quickly, and I got my left and right hands mixed up. "I'm not very good," I said.

"No," he agreed—but without sounding mean about it. "You don't seem to have the hang of it yet. Do you want to go for a walk instead? There's a skate park up the road. We could just hang out there for a while and watch? Leave these two getting to know each other better."

"That'd be great!"

I'd never walked to a skate park to just hang out with a guy before. But Cal seemed to take it in his stride.

"That was pretty cool," he said, "what you did for your dad. What exactly made you do it?"

"I thought he was depressed," I said. "I got worried, you know. You read about middle-aged men who have lost everything doing something stupid."

"But he's got a veggie garden," Cal pointed out. "Gardeners don't tend to be stupid people. They like seeing their crops come up, or planning for next season's planting."

"I should have thought of that," I said.

"Oh, well, you're probably younger than I am."

It turned out I was only two years younger than Cal. The perfect age gap, according to some magazine I'd read. He didn't even have much acne. Of course, he wasn't Richard. He seemed much more serious and didn't joke around like Richard. But that also meant that he didn't tease me the way Richard did. He listened to me talk about the Chronicles, and then he told me who his favorite fantasy writer was, and he didn't call me Magwheels once.

We hung out for so long that Dad and Spooky came to find us.

"We thought you'd run away with the circus," Dad said. "Time to go now, Magenta. I've invited Lianna back for some cold chicken and salad—the tomatoes this season have been sensational, Lianna—and you should taste these heirloom ones I've planted. They are the best—aren't they, Magenta?"

"They're really sweet," I agreed. Spooky was coming for dinner, which meant Cal was coming for dinner. That was a step in exactly the right direction. I beamed at Dad, but he just smiled blandly back at me.

Spooky took off her high-heeled sandals so she could march out to the backyard, where she oohed and ahhed over our veggie patch.

"And you dug it up from scratch, Max. That's amazing. I wouldn't know where to put something like that."

"You just watch the sun," Dad explained. "You pick the sunniest spot. It's pretty easy, Lianna. If you wanted to do something like this, I'd be happy to help."

"It's just a wasted effort in a rental," Spooky said. "You never know when you might have to move. That's the only thing I hate. The last place? We were there for two years, really settled. Then the landlady's daughter came back from overseas. It was awful, wasn't it, Cal?"

Cal shrugged and stubbed the ground with his foot. "It wasn't that bad," he said.

"Some suburbs have community gardens," Dad said. "I've been hassling the council about doing something like that here. It would bring the community together more. Particularly now that so many people, like yourself, are forced to rent."

"Oh, Max, you're so full of great ideas. I can't

understand why someone as creative as you hasn't just walked into a terrific job. The workplace needs people like you."

Dad shrugged and looked away to the horizon. "I've got some ideas," he said. "I'm thinking—but it's a bit premature to talk about it. I've been doing some research, though."

"I just don't know how you find the time," Spooky said, gazing at the veggie garden as though it was some kind of shrine. "It seems to me that I scarcely get the place clean, go to the gym—I do believe in keeping up one's physical health—and then Cal's home with his demands. Then I cook dinner, and that's practically my day. Gone.

"Oh, and on Thursdays and Fridays, I help out at my friend's café. I'm also part of a women's group. We meet every other week."

"You sound pretty busy to me." Dad smiled at her. "It sounds like a full kind of life."

"Well, not completely." Spooky glanced at him very quickly and then went back to staring at the veggie garden.

"Come on, then," Dad said, "let's pick some of these beautiful tomatoes. Magenta, grab a head of lettuce, will you?"

"I'll make the salad," Spooky said, once we'd brought it all into the kitchen. "Do you have any eggs, Max? And olive oil? I'll make fresh mayonnaise."

"We've got some mayo in the fridge," I told her. "That stuff that's ninety-eight percent fat-free with no added sugar?"

"That's not mayonnaise." Spooky smiled at me and patted my arm. "That stuff is to real mayonnaise like a

Harlequin Romance is to real passion. You just wait until you taste my mayo. You won't want that chemically enhanced glue ever again!"

Spooky's mayo took about half an hour to make. She needed an electric blender, but of course we didn't have one.

"That's a shame," she said. "Some electrical goods are worth hanging on to, Max. Pumpkin soup is a winter standby for us, isn't it, Cal? No blender, no pumpkin soup!"

"You can always have lumpy pumpkin soup," my dad said. He was looking through the bottom drawer, trying to find a whisk. "Here, is this what you want?"

"Hmm. That should do it. It'll be a bit more work, but it's worth it. Sometimes doing things the old-fashioned way is good for the soul. Perhaps you're right about the soup. You could always use a potato masher, I guess. Here goes. Now, the trick is to trickle that oil in so slowly it doesn't have a chance to curdle. . . ."

Spooky's mayo was fine—but it lacked a certain something.

When I told Polly later, she knew immediately. "Sugar— that's what it was missing. Chemically enhanced glue, as she called it, always has sugar in it. To make you like it. What you had was the proper thing, Magenta. Which, as the daughter of a caterer, I can assure you is better than the premade stuff."

"Well, I didn't think so."

"Anyway, what was she like? Do you think they'll fall in love?"

"They didn't eat much," I said. "Well, they ate lots of

lettuce and cucumber and tomatoes, but they didn't want any chicken, really, although Cal had a piece and Spooky picked at the stuffing. Dad kept saying it was free-range chicken, and Spooky said, 'Well, if it's free-range . . .' and put another piece on Cal's plate and frowned at him. Then they talked about grown-up stuff. World issues. Or rather Dad talked, and Spooky listened."

"What's the boy like?"

"He's great. He's really cool, actually. He reads a lot and doesn't like sports except for swimming and tennis. I can't play tennis, but he offered to teach me one day. He hasn't any acne at all, and he has these great, long eyes."

"Sounds weird," Polly said. "Long eyes?"

"You know—big eyes but not round. Long-big."

"Gee, Magenta, you may need to reconsider your chosen career—I don't think much of that description."

"He's kind of cute," I said.

"A good practice boy, then," she said, "like Hentley?"

I was saving the best news for last, but I was tempted not to tell Polly because she was being so strange. But I couldn't keep secrets. I was hopeless. "The best thing is that we're all going camping two weekends from now. Cal will be there, because it's partly for him that we're going. Spooky's got this real thing about male role models. She doesn't want him to miss out on anything just because he's living with her and not his dad."

"I'll make a love potion," Polly said immediately. "Everything will be fine."

"I don't want a love potion. I mean, I'm not sure that I like him that much, and anyway, it feels like cheating."

"Not for you, you dope. For your dad and Spooky."

"Oh." I blushed, even though there was no one to see me. "Yes, of course. Sorry."

"So you do like him, then!"

"Well, sure, because he listens, Polly, and he's got this little smile. He's really nice. But that's all."

"Time will tell," Polly said with her irritating superior air, "time and camping. If you can go camping with someone and come out the other side still liking them, it's a done thing."

"What do you mean?"

"Oh, get real, Magenta. Camping? No showers. Or if there are showers, no hot water. Or they're just too far away to bother with. Twigs in your hair. No mirror, so you can't see the twigs, or the fact that your face is all creased right through breakfast. You start to smell, and your hair goes oily. A mosquito bite on your face gets infected and looks like the world's biggest pimple, and every time you tell anyone it's just a bug bite they go, 'Oh, yeah, sure.' Someone who won't be mentioned forgets to bring the olive oil, so all the gourmet fat-free sausages burn and stick to the metal barbecue, which you didn't like the idea of anyway, because how would you know it was really clean?"

"Okay, okay. It won't be that bad. I've been camping with Dad lots of times, and nothing like that happens. I can take a mirror—there's even a little place in our tent to hang it. We take bug spray. And Dad never buys fat-free sausages. Ever."

"It's your funeral," Polly said grimly. "I hope he's worth it."

"It's not about Cal," I said. "It's about Spooky and Dad

getting together and being happy for the rest of their lives."

"Then you'll have to eat proper French mayo forever," Polly said.

She did love getting the last word.

# Plump Roses and Revision

Mom asked me questions about Spooky all week. Was she skinny or plump? What did she do? What color was her hair? Was it dyed? Oh, and did I like her? Oh, and why did she call herself Spooky?

"She's in-between. I don't know. Blondish. She doesn't call herself Spooky; it was sort of a joke. Cal said it would scare losers away. But Mom, we hardly know her," I said for the umpteenth time. "Honestly." I had decided to avoid telling Mom my whole role in the Spooky affair. I didn't exactly lie, but I certainly made it sound as though Dad had put his profile on the Internet himself.

"Of course everyone is doing it these days," Mom said. "You read about it all the time in the paper. I say, good for him. About time." But she didn't sound as though she entirely meant it. We were having a late pancake breakfast. Trib was out of town again, and Mom had splurged on real maple syrup and trashy magazines.

"You've got Trib," I pointed out. "You're getting married. Dad should at least go on a date."

"Did I say he shouldn't?" Mom asked.

"Nooo, but you didn't sound as glad as you might have. After all, he sent you a congratulations card when you and Trib got engaged." Actually, Dad didn't send the card, I did. I forged his handwriting. I was used to doing that, because he always forgot the field trip permission forms on his week.

"Did he?" Mom sounded vague. She turned on the electric blender, and the noise filled the kitchen.

"You know he did," I said when she stopped the mixer. "You even said how generous it was."

"I can't remember now," Mom lied. "Lots of people sent cards. That's what people do. I am glad for your dad; of course I am. I'm just . . . wondering what's she's like, that's all. Dad must have been curious about Trib."

"He met him," I pointed out to her. "He met Trib because he had to drop me off early. Remember? Trib was wearing a towel. They tried to shake hands?"

Mom's mouth twitched. "You're right," she said. "It's high time your dad went on a date. Even if it is a camping date."

"I think camping's great. Mom, I really need a new pair of running shoes. Really, really. I'm thinking of getting serious about running, and good running shoes help you . . . run." I was hoping to get Mom in a shopping mood while Trib was away. There were heaps of things I needed for the camping trip if I was going to look sophisticated and avoid camp tackiness.

"Of course," Mom said without much enthusiasm. "Running shoes for running. Let's eat first, okay?"

She cheered up over pancakes, and by the time we'd loaded the dishwasher, she'd started a shopping list. We hit the stores just before lunch. It's the ideal time to start shopping, because you do a little before hunger strikes, then you take a break and return with renewed energy.

Mom was looking for something garden-partyish for the wedding. While she did that, I was keeping an eye out for camp essentials, like a simple but stylish three-quarter-sleeve black top, denim shorts or cutoff jeans, and new pj's. Definitely new pj's. I wasn't going to be seen dead or alive in my old teddy-bear ones that I kept at Dad's. I needed Felix the Cat ones. Eventually, after Mom had tried on three hundred skirts, not one of which was perfect, I steered her into the pj's section.

"I need new ones," I said. "Really, truly. For the camping trip."

"Isn't that your dad's responsibility?" Mom asked. Her face looked pink in an irritated way. "Did you think I looked, um . . . plumpish in that skirt with roses? Like, really plumpish?"

"No," I said for the thousandth time, "I didn't think you looked plump, not even slightly plumpish. The rose skirt was my personal favorite. But when I said that, you said the roses were too plump."

"Maybe it wasn't the roses. I was just projecting plumpness onto them. I'm never going to find anything to wear for this wedding."

"Pajamas . . ."

"For the camping trip? Are you crazy? Just wear your old ones."

"I can't."

"Oh, Magenta, why not? I've already bought running shoes, a black top (though I really do think you're too young for a black top), and shorts (even though it must be the end of summer soon), and now you want pajamas."

"Her son is coming," I said finally.

"Her son?" Mom raised an eyebrow. "That's very family oriented."

"Well, we are. Aren't we? I mean we were, and now you are and Dad is. In separate ways."

Mom's mouth set in a grim line. "So you want new pajamas because this Lianna's son is going to accompany you all camping. How old is he?"

"About my age. Mom, stop it. You're just doing this because you don't want Dad to go on a date."

"I didn't know the date involved children," Mom said. "I suppose I should be pleased about such an inclusive policy, but I kind of thought they'd date quietly before involving everyone else."

"Right. Like you and Trib?"

"That was your dad's fault for dropping you off early. If that hadn't happened, you would have met Trib when I was ready for it, not accidentally like that. I was very upset about it all."

"So you mean you would have kept Trib from me? Isn't that kind of lying?"

"No. No, it isn't. It's just sensible. You don't know how these things will turn out. People, kids, can get hurt. Imagine if you'd liked Trib and were imagining him as a kind of stepdad figure, while Trib and I were busy trying to extricate ourselves from the relationship. There's a right time to do things, Magenta. I'm surprised at your father, really."

I ended up with Felix pajamas anyway. They were on sale, and even Mom admitted they were cute.

"Just don't think that every time your dad goes out with someone, it means you can get a complete change of wardrobe," Mom warned. "I'm not made of money, you know."

"I won't; really, I won't. This time was special. Thanks, Mom."

"So what's this woman's son like?"

"Okay. Pretty cool."

"Pretty cool?" Mom raised one eyebrow. I think she learned that when she learned to be a teacher. I'd tried for hours to do it, but it never worked for me.

"You know, for a boy."

"Right. As a species they tend to be very uncool," Mom said.

"You know, they talk about football and stuff." I was squirming and trying not to look as though I was. "He looks like Spook . . . I mean Lianna." I offered Mom a distraction.

"So what does he look like?"

"He's got these long eyes. They're kind of unusual." There was that eyebrow again.

"Unusual good or unusual bad?"

"Good," I said, after pretending to think about it for a second.

"That's a plus. Any other distinguishing features?"

"Curly hair."

"Long or short?"

"Kind of in-between." I was confused as to whether we were talking about Cal or Spooky.

"So would you call her attractive?"

"Her? Oh, sure, yeah, she's okay, you know. A bit old, but okay."

"How old? Do you think, for example, she's my age? Or is she younger?"

"I don't know, Mom. What does it matter?"

"I'm just curious, that's all. If this woman is going to be your stepmother—"

"They've had coffee, that's all, Mom!"

"Sorry. New topic. Do you want to pick up some sushi to take home for dinner?"

"Isn't the rice a hotbed for bacterial growth?" That was Mom's favorite line about sushi takeout.

"Yeah, it is, but let's risk it this time, hey? I don't feel much like cooking. Those pancakes used up all my cooking energy."

"She's a great cook," I told Mom over sushi takeout. She'd been obsessing about the plump roses again, but that's not why I said it. It was because we were smearing mayonnaise on our heated-up Japanese omelets. It was Japanese mayonnaise, but it still reminded me of Spooky.

"Is she?" Mom's voice sounded a little arctic.

"She made mayo from scratch. With a whisk."

"She found a whisk in your father's kitchen? That surprises me."

"You took the blender," I pointed out.

"Your father didn't use it. Not in my day," Mom snapped. "Sorry, Magenta. Can we just leave Lianna out of our evening for a while?"

"You keep bringing her up," I protested.

"You did that time."

"But every other time you did."

"Okay, well, I've stopped now. Let's watch television?"

The movie didn't help. It was some crummy romantic thing about a couple meeting somewhere exotic after they'd divorced years back and falling in love all over again.

"Dreadful mush," Mom said, but she didn't turn it off. I was tired, but I ended up watching the whole movie with her in solidarity. It didn't make sense to me that she was cranky with Dad for going out with Spooky, but she was my mom, and even though we'd snapped at each other and she'd asked stupid questions, I loved her.

"I think it's silly marrying someone you've divorced," I told her after the movie ended with the couple in church again getting married with their old bridesmaids and best man.

"It's a bit repetitive. But I suppose if you've both learned something from the experience . . . Anyway, it's just a movie. I don't think that happens much in real life. I mean, why bother?"

"Would you marry Dad again?" I asked her when she came in to kiss me good night.

"Good heavens, no!" she said briskly, pulling the sheet right up to my chin. "As if I could do that! We spent today looking for a garden-party skirt for my next wedding."

"That doesn't sound right," I said sleepily. "It sounds

as though you're going to get married over and over and over again like a celebrity."

"I'm not! It's hard enough to find the right outfit once. Twice is pushing it, and I wouldn't have a hope in hell the third time." I opened my eyes, but she was grinning. "Of course it's not about what you wear, Magenta. It's about love. I want to look good, too, though. I want to be a beautiful bride. Do you think those roses were too plump?"

"You could always go on a diet," I said, "just for the wedding. Then the plump roses wouldn't matter, because they'd be covering a skinnier you."

"I could." She sighed. "No more pancakes. No more Japanese omelets. No more mayo. No more ice cream at the movies. No more popcorn while we watch DVDs. I could go on a diet."

"It would be a limited-lifespan diet," I said, "and therefore easier to manage. Plus you can still eat popcorn, just not the buttery kind."

"Maybe I could get a vertically striped garden-party skirt. Vertical stripes are thin by their very nature."

"Not flowery, though."

"Flowery might be overrated. Perhaps we should have more of a geometric garden party, you know, with checkerboard-iced cupcakes and rather severe leafy arrangements."

"Sounds . . . unusual."

"Unusual good or bad?"

"Mom, stick with the flowers, please? I don't think

Trib's going to take any radical changes that well. He liked the garden-party idea. You were going to get a hat. You'll find the perfect skirt."

"Maybe. Maybe not."

She sounded so dejected that I gave her an extra hug. Really, being a daughter could be exhausting sometimes. Still, it did give me a good idea for the next bit of the Chronicles. A much-needed good idea.

> *Holly woke up with a start. Was that Eclipse coming back? How would the cat get hold of a key, though? the young witch wondered sleepily.*
>
> *"Psst, are you awake?"*
>
> *"Yessss, more or less," Holly said, blinded by the light. "Who is it?"*
>
> *"It's Lady Burgundy," the light bearer answered. "I just want to know some things."*
>
> *Holly smoothed down her tunic and sat straighter against the cold, damp stones.*
>
> *"Why do you think I should tell you?" she demanded, all sleepiness gone.*
>
> *"Because it might be worth your while," the silky voice answered softly.*
>
> *"Might?"*
>
> *"Might." The voice was crisp now. "I can't make any promises."*
>
> *"What do you want to know?"*
>
> *"Where did you see my . . . um . . . my first husband?"*
>
> *"In my scriving bowl," Holly answered.*

"Not the bowl, you stupid little thing! Where was he? In what country? What land? Was he with anyone or was he alone?"

"I don't know where it was," Holly answered haughtily. "The bowl didn't mention a location."

"With anyone? A woman?" Lady Burgundy leaned against the opposite wall, still holding the lamp, which shone directly into Holly's eyes. She was pretending to be casual, Holly was sure. She wasn't the kind of lady to go tramping down dungeons in the middle of the night unless there was something she really wanted to know.

"There were people with him," Holly said cautiously.

"Men? Women?"

"A mixture," the apprentice witch said, "I think."

"You think? Don't you know?" The voice was no longer silky. It was razor sharp.

"I was more focused on Lord Burgundy, if you please. After all, he was the one supposed to be dead, Your Ladyship."

"Still, if you think back, you'll remember." The voice became coaxing again.

Holly thought. She could remember Lord Burgundy, leaning on some kind of statue thing, and a group of people pressing around him. Someone stood close to him, but man or woman? She squinted against the light. Long hair, she remembered, long dark hair and some silver flashing at a slender throat.

"A woman," she said slowly. "Standing next to him."

"Young or old?"

"Young enough to have hair as brown as dead leaves."

"You mean no gray?" Even in the dark, Lady Burgundy put her hand up to her own hair. She used an expensive dye from bark and berries found in the woods. It gave her hair a reddish tinge that was often admired and that looked quite natural.

"None at all." Holly stared past the light at Lady Burgundy. Now that her eyes were getting used to the light, she could see the older woman quite well. Her sharp witch's eyes saw the gray beginning to show at the roots of the red hair. "She was thin, too," she added for good measure, "wearing a lot of jewelry." She watched Lady Burgundy's eyes narrow. That will show her, Holly thought. That will teach her to lock up one of the Wood People.

Lady Burgundy stood there, holding her candle. A cold anger crossed her face like a storm across the sea.

"I think you need to spend more time in your own company," she said. "Think things over. I'll talk to you again when you've had a chance to gain some new insights."

"But you said—"

"I said 'might.' Remember that word? It usually means no. Or didn't your mother teach you anything?" With that, Lady Burgundy whirled out of the dank cell, slamming the door behind her and leaving the place even darker than it had seemed before. The scuffling rats sounded closer, and Holly bit back a sob. Why hadn't she told Lady Burgundy all she knew? Why?

I didn't know the answer myself, but I figured it would come to me. I was beginning to like Holly more than I had expected to. Did that kind of thing happen often to writers, I wondered? Both Holly and Lady Burgundy were a little more interesting than Lady Rosa, which wasn't really fair, as she was the one trying to be good. It was just that the whole kissing-parapet thing was going on for too long. It wasn't her fault; it was mine. I vowed to rescue her even if it meant she spurned Ricardo. It was weird that when I thought of her saying no to Ricardo, it made her that little bit more intriguing. After all, what girl in her right mind would say no to Ricardo? He had everything. He was rich, good-looking, strong and brave, and just flirty enough. Maybe she could see some kind of shadow no one else could. Or maybe she'd feel it when they kissed?

I thought I'd sleep on it. I didn't want to make any big mistakes. I didn't want to have to revise anything. Writing it down once was hard enough. It was sort of like marriage. I'd want to get that right the first time, too, if I could. Look what Mom was going through just trying to get a thin skirt. I knew she hadn't had to think of vertical stripes the first time. I'd seen the photos of her and Dad, even though she'd hidden them in the store room. They'd been wedding-y with lots of lace and roses and not a stripe anywhere. She'd smiled nervously and beautifully and Dad had held her hand. They'd looked fresh and young until life had revised them. I was against revision. It hurt too much.

# Camping

I expected Dad to be in a great mood when I went back to his place. With the camping trip coming up, he had lots to do to keep his mind off any of his problems. Not to mention the fact that he and Spooky had been in almost daily communication about the trip—where to go, when to leave, what clothes to bring, and so forth.

I heard this from Cal, who talked to me on MSN. He didn't talk every day like a boyfriend or anything. We just happened to be online at the same time a couple of days. He told me that Spooky kicked him off the computer regularly so she could talk to Dad.

So it was a complete surprise when I got to Dad's place to discover him grumping around.

"What is it?" I asked when the banging and swearing from the garage became too much to ignore.

"This camping trip is getting out of hand." Dad glared at me as though it was all my fault. "It's bad timing, too. In fact, the timing couldn't be worse."

"Why? We weren't doing anything. We never do anything." I normally didn't like to rub it in, but when he pushed me to the edge like this, I could play dirty.

"Well, it just may be that some of us had plans for that weekend."

"You had plans? Then why did you make it that weekend? You set the date."

He glared at me again. "The plans came up after the original plan."

"That doesn't make sense," I pointed out. "You can't have plans come up after other plans. You could have—I don't know—ideas, maybe? Anyway, how is that my fault, and what was the other idea?"

"Nothing. Don't worry about it. It wouldn't have worked out anyway, probably." Dad sounded a bit sheepish. "I suppose you're right, Magenta. It was my fault for agreeing to go in the first place."

"I don't get it." I drew up a milk crate and sat down on it. "You were the one who suggested going. I thought I'd come home and you'd be cheerful and smiling and busy."

"I am busy." Dad waved at the growing pile of equipment. "You've got to admit I'm busy."

"I wanted you to be cheerfully busy." I felt my bottom lip wobble a bit and my chin crease.

"Oh, Mags." Dad came over and put his hand on my shoulder. "I'm sorry. I am looking forward to camping. Truly. It's just that something came up, and I'm a bit worried that I've given Lianna the wrong impression. It's a difficult situation."

"I don't understand what's difficult," I said stubbornly. "It's just a friendly camping trip."

"I hope so," Dad said, patting my shoulder. "I really hope so."

I was looking forward to camping. By Wednesday I had packed practically everything I was taking. I'd recharged batteries for my flashlight, my camera, and my old MP3 player. I'd supervised Dad making toasted muesli, making sure he didn't add anything I detested, like sunflower seeds or dried banana. I'd found my old slippers, which was quite a feat, as I'd taken them off in the backyard behind the compost bin. I'd picked the slugs off them and dried them out in the laundry. I'd even found my best hat. I'd checked essentials like sunblock, bug spray, and lavender oil in case I did get bitten by anything and also to make me smell okay, despite sketchy showers. I'd bought twenty-four-hour-strength deodorant. I was prepared.

It was weird that I hadn't heard from Cal all week. I kept expecting him to pop up, so I kept the computer on for longer than I normally would, but no Cal, and no Lianna, either. That had Dad scratching his head a bit.

"Maybe we should call?" I said.

"I've only got a cell number," Dad said. "I've already tried it. Out of range or turned off."

"Maybe they've lost the charger?"

"Maybe they've left town." Dad sounded gloomy. "We've done all this for nothing."

"I wouldn't mind going camping with just us," I told him, even though my heart sank at the thought of Cal not seeing me in my new Felix pajamas.

"Why, of course. I didn't mean that," Dad said, but he wasn't as convincing as he could have been.

"I bet that's what's happened—they're so busy trying to pack everything that they're not getting onto the computer at all, and they've lost the cell phone charger," I said heartily, but a bit of me could imagine Spooky packing up her small dilapidated car with all their belongings and fleeing. Not from Dad, but from something else. A wicked landlord or a fight with the friend who ran the café.

On Thursday I got a text message on my cell. It read: *All set 4 sat am do we bring anything?* I showed Dad the text. He dictated the reply to me: *We have everything under control equip-wise. u handle food as agreed. c u 8am.*

"Maybe she's been testing recipes? Maybe that's why we haven't heard anything until now?"

He shook his head. "It'll be something messier," he said. "Lianna's one of those people, Magenta. Life's never straightforward."

"Cal's pretty level-headed."

"One of them has to be," Dad said.

"She's a good cook, though," I pointed out.

"She's a good person," Dad said, "but that doesn't mean that things aren't messy at her end. That probably wasn't even her cell. It certainly wasn't the number she gave me."

On Friday afternoon Dad and I packed the car. Dad was very particular about packing and knew just what went where to maximize space, keep balanced, and minimize the risk of flying objects. When we were finished, he rubbed his hands.

"Ha!" he said. "Pretty good job, Magenta. There's still room for a couple of sleeping bags, packs, and cooler. That'll be all they'll need, and we've got legroom, too. Let's order out pizza, eh? Last meal in civilization."

We ate in front of the television and watched one of those English murder shows where brutal murders are committed every week in a pretty little village. I went to bed early. I didn't want to have shadows under my eyes at the start of the trip.

Spooky and Cal arrived at a quarter to eight the next morning. Dad was still shaving, but we'd had reheated pizza leftovers, and Dad had already made a thermos of coffee.

"You answer it!" he yelled when the doorbell sounded. "That'll be them."

Spooky had bags under her eyes. She was already smiling when I opened the door, but it was a thin smile that hovered nervously around her mouth.

"Sorry," she said even before she'd said hello. "Sorry, we're a bit early, I know."

"That's okay. Hi, Cal."

Cal grunted and nodded at me. Not a morning person. Neither of them were, to judge from their appearances. His hair was wildly all over the place, and he had his sweater on inside out. I wondered how, or if, I was going to tell him.

"So glad you got the text message. Cal's was the only phone working. It's been quite a week, hasn't it, Cal? Still, we got here in the end, and that's what's important, isn't it? Where shall I put these, Magenta?"

I looked down. Between them they had three long tote bags, four of those supermarket green bags overflowing with groceries, a pillow, and the largest cooler I had ever seen. It looked quite new.

"Umm, better wait for Dad. He's the packing expert." I wasn't sure where it was all going to go, but I was pretty certain that Dad hadn't factored in four supermarket bags that looked as though they had to be kept upright.

Dad huffed and puffed when he saw it all, but as Spooky pointed out, we did have a big car.

"Last vestige of a previous life," Dad told her, rearranging things. "I only kept it for this kind of trip."

"It's fantastic," Spooky said. "I bet it's got a CD player."

"Of course." Dad shrugged. "But the main thing is the high suspension."

"High suspension?"

"You can get this monster in where you wouldn't dare put another car that wasn't a four-wheel drive."

"It's not a four-wheel drive?"

"God, no. I wouldn't have one of those things in the city. My ex wanted one, but—"

"Mom said why not go all out?" I interrupted. "Then we'd never get stuck again. We got stuck in the mud," I told Spooky. "It took hours for anyone to come to dig us out. That's why Mom wanted a four-wheel drive."

"It's a great car," Spooky said. "Heavens, I don't even have air-conditioning."

We all turned automatically to look at Spooky's car. It was old, and someone had rammed the back of it. You didn't need to know anything about cars to realize that it wouldn't have a CD player in it.

"So long as it goes," Dad said heartily. "Shall we, folks?"

As soon as we piled into the backseat, Cal brought out an MP3 player and offered me one of his earphones.

"Dad doesn't like me listening in the car," I said.

"He and Mom are getting to know each other," Cal said, not even bothering to whisper. "It'll be fine. I've got some good music on this."

Cal's version of what was good music seemed to be a bit hippieish to me, but you could hear all the lyrics, which was unusual, and I liked that. I kept one ear on Dad and Spooky's conversation for a while, but it was pretty boring. Dad talked about the traffic, the weather, and environmental issues. Spooky talked about her work in the café and organic food. They didn't seem to be talking to each other, exactly. I figured they were happy, so eventually I took out my book and read, which was what Cal was doing. I was pleased I'd put it in my backpack. Normally Dad won't allow reading in the car, either. I have to either talk to him or look at the scenery. They're the car-trip rules. Dad wasn't paying any attention to the rules because he had Spooky to deal with. The label on her top was sticking out, and I thought I should tuck it in for her, the way my mother would have. But I didn't feel I knew her well enough to say "Your tag is showing" and maybe put my fingers on the powdery skin of her neck.

We only went as far as Wilson's Prom—about a two-hour

trip. Usually Dad and I go farther. When he and Mom were still together, they'd drive for hours. I'd be bundled into the car half-asleep, and by the time I woke up, we'd be somewhere completely strange and still driving. They'd swap, taking turns to drive. The one who wasn't driving got to choose the CDs. I liked it best when Dad drove, because Mom would put music on we could both sing along to. I knew Dad thought Wilson's Prom was a beginner's camp, but I didn't say anything as Spooky got out and stretched her legs, declaring how beautiful it all was.

"There are March flies," I warned her. "They don't respect bug spray." I was already on the lookout. I hate March flies worst, sandflies second, and mosquitoes third.

"The whole experience," Spooky said brightly. "Cal—we'll be experienced campers after this."

"Here you are, young man." Dad threw Cal our hiking tent. "Have a go at putting that up. Just give us a yell if you need a hand. Magenta, come over here and help Lianna."

I spent the next half an hour running between Dad, Lianna, and Cal. Dad and I were the only ones who had a clue. Lianna put the wrong pole through the front loops, and her tent went up lopsided, which she didn't even seem to notice until Dad pointed it out.

"Wrong pole," he said. "This'd just fall over in a storm." He poked the tent, and it lurched to one side.

"Goodness," Spooky said. "I thought I'd followed the instructions." I was going to laugh, but when I looked at her, her chin seemed to be wobbling almost as badly as the tent.

"Everyone makes mistakes the first time," I said. "I should have picked that up. After all, I was helping."

"Okay, girls," Dad said. "Magenta, that's the longest pole, and it goes straight through the middle. Can you work it out? I'll set up the stove and make us all a cup of tea."

When we were finished, we had a decent campsite. Dad and I had the biggest tent, of course, because we were sharing. I didn't mind sharing with Dad. I slept in the space that would normally have stored the luggage but was quite big enough for one person. It was cozy. I'd already spread out my sleeping bag and put my flashlight and book in the special net pocket so I'd have no trouble finding them in the dark. My pack was neatly at the bottom of the sleeping bag, and my pj's were on top.

The others were drinking tea and discussing what they wanted to do. Or rather, Dad and Cal were. Spooky was just nodding and smiling while she looked around nervously.

"My sleeping bag's already out," I said, taking a cup of tea from Dad and putting in a bit too much sugar, which was allowed when you were camping.

"Good for you," Dad said.

"Oh, that's what we'll have to get from you, Max, sleeping bags."

"Sleeping bags?" Dad echoed.

Spooky nodded. She was sitting on the edge of her camp chair as though she was scared it would break if she leaned back. She looked so uncomfortable it made me feel fidgety.

"You didn't bring any?" Dad asked.

"You said you'd bring all the equipment," Spooky said. "I brought food in a cooler. That was the arrangement. Wasn't it?"

"Sleeping bags aren't really equipment," Dad said. "They're kind of essential. I assumed you'd bring sleeping bags, just like you brought a pillow."

"I thought they were equipment," Spooky said. "Anyway, we couldn't have brought them, because we don't have any."

"They'd have to count as equipment," Cal said, watching his mother. "They're not standard. They're camping gear, and that equals equipment. At home we sleep on mattresses, between sheets and under blankets."

"Okay," Dad said, "okay. So we're down two sleeping bags. That's a problem."

"Is there a camping store anywhere?" I asked.

"That's your mother's kind of solution," Dad said. "I don't think Lianna can afford to suddenly shell out for two sleeping bags, and I know I can't."

"It's not my mother's," I said, stung. "It was just an idea, that's all."

"Well, not a very practical one. Did anyone bring a blanket?"

"I did, sort of," Spooky said. "It's not very big, and I only brought it because, well, I don't really know why, but I put it in at the last minute. I had this feeling. You know, how you suddenly get feelings."

"So we've got two sleeping bags and one blanket," Dad said. "Okay. I can sleep in my clothes. Lianna, you can have my sleeping bag; Magenta keeps hers, and Cal has the blanket."

"Oh, no," Spooky said, "I'll take the blanket. Cal can have the sleeping bag."

"Don't be stupid, Mom," Cal said. "You're taking the sleeping bag. Don't argue about it."

I looked at Cal with new respect. I would have accepted the sleeping bag in a heartbeat.

"It's all right," Dad said too cheerfully. "We've all got ground sheets, it's summer, and this is luxury compared to . . ." He trailed off, obviously thinking.

"Africa," I said. It's always Africa. "You know, Dad, there might be a mat or something in the bottom of the trunk, too. Remember? From that meditation class you did?"

There was a small argument about who took the mat. Cal wanted Dad to take it, and Dad wanted Cal to take it. I nearly offered to take it and save them the debate. I knew from experience that I'd wake up and have some big stone lodged under my back.

"I'm so sorry," Spooky kept saying. "I just really didn't think that sleeping bags weren't part of camping equipment. I mean, what else would you want them for?"

Eventually Cal gave her a look and said, "Shut up, Mom," but in quite a nice voice. She shut her mouth quickly as though swallowing an unpleasant pill.

Then we all went to the beach. We had just enough time for a surf before lunch, Dad said, even though my stomach was rumbling.

At first it was really awkward. I mean, you don't really

want to see anyone you know while you're wearing a wet suit, do you? They're so . . . industrial. I didn't want to wear one, but Dad insisted, even when I pointed out that Cal didn't have one. He was in board shorts and a surf shirt that was wearing thin.

"That's their business," he hissed. "I can't help their equipment beyond what I've already done. You are wearing your wet suit, Magenta, and that's that."

"C'mon, then, last one in's a rotten egg," Dad called. He was wearing a wet suit, and his old man's stomach poked out like a little pouch. His shoulders were still a little broader than Cal's, though. "Lianna, you're coming in, aren't you?"

Spooky had taken her skirt off. Her legs were vanilla-ice-cream white. She'd put on a huge straw hat, and underneath that her long-sleeved black T-shirt made her look like a strange bicolored spider.

"Not yet," she said. "I need some time."

Dad shrugged, but I was intrigued. What did she need time for? The water wasn't going to get warmer or calmer. This was it.

"Just to . . . you know . . . do it," she said apologetically. "I wasn't a sporty kind of kid."

"That's okay, Mom," Cal said. "You can stay out here and sunbathe if you want."

"Oh, no, I don't want to do that," Spooky said. "Skin cancer, Cal. Why do you think I smear so much expensive sunblock over myself?"

"Sorry, Mom, I was just trying—"

"You all go in. I'm fine. I love sitting on the beach,

watching. This little sun tent is a really good thing, Max. It's wonderful how prepared you are."

The water was freezing. I was glad to be wearing my wet suit. I got a couple of good waves with my board, and Cal turned out to be a pretty good bodysurfer.

"This is great, isn't it?" Dad said, coming up behind us on his board. "Isn't this great, kids? Why won't your mom come in, Cal? She doesn't know what she's missing."

Cal shrugged. "I don't think she gets the whole swimming thing. She'll be okay on the beach. She'll probably go for a walk or something."

Sure enough, when we finally got out, Spooky was sitting in the beach tent beside a huge pile of little shells. She looked happier.

"I'm going to take these home," she said, scooping the shells up into her hat.

"What are you going to do with them?" I asked. I had a jar of shells from my last camping trip, but I'd never figured out what to do with them.

"I'm not sure. Maybe decorate a picture frame? I know it sounds a bit kitschy, but kitsch is in at the moment, isn't it? I was thinking of making some of those softies, you know. I might use some of the shells for eyes."

"Softies?"

"Those little soft toys the kids are crazy about these days. They're kind of cute. I was thinking of trying to make some and sell them. Just for some pocket money."

"That's a great idea," I said. I'd just figured out what she was talking about. "You can make really evil ones, too, you know. A girl at my school is collecting them."

"I'm not sure that I want to make evil ones," Spooky said. "There's already so much bad in the world. Soft toys should be sweet, I think, not evil."

"Evil ones might sell better." Cal had folded the tent up all by himself, without being asked. I could tell Dad was impressed.

"Do you think so?"

"Yes," Cal said firmly, "I do. They're more novel than the sweet ones. I tell you what, Mom, why don't you do evil ones but dress them really sweetly?"

"Cool." I could see them in my mind. They'd have little stitched scars and screaming mouths, but they'd be wearing pale pink skirts with rosebuds and ruffles.

"I'll have to see," Spooky said. "It was just a little idea I had, Cal. If you know so much about these, maybe you should make them."

"I can't sew," Cal said. "You know that. I could design them, though. You could make them up from my designs. After all, I know more about the teen market than you do."

"A mother-and-son enterprise," Dad said. "I like it. It's a good hook, too."

Spooky looked flustered. "You're right," she said. "But Cal, you have to study. You can't spend your spare time designing softies."

"How much time can it take?" Cal asked. "Let's do a couple, okay, Mom? See what happens. It doesn't have to be a big thing."

"Can we eat?" I was starving.

"Of course, darling," Spooky said. "We'll go back to the campsite and have a delicious lunch. Let's talk about business another time."

I was a bit doubtful about Spooky's definition of delicious when it turned out we were going to have salad sandwiches. One of the rules of camping was that you didn't have to have healthy meals. No one had told Spooky, obviously. However, the sandwiches were scrumptious.

"These are excellent," Dad said, examining his sandwich. "I've got to hand it to you, Lianna. This is the best camping lunch I've ever had!"

"Why, thanks, Max. The trick is the pesto, of course. Gives it that oomph."

Jane, Polly's Mom, would like Spooky. They'd be able to talk food together. I'd have to see how I could get them together. Maybe I could just outright ask Jane to invite Spooky and my dad over to dinner. That way Polly could cast one of her love spells then and there. It wasn't a bad idea. I was beginning to like Spooky. Although I was also beginning to really like Cal. That kind of complicated things.

"Magenta and I'll clean up," Cal offered. "Why don't you two go for a walk or something?"

"You sure?" Spooky said. "I don't mind, honestly."

"No, go on. You prepared the sandwiches. Why don't you both go and get a coffee or something? There's a shop."

I stared at Cal. What was he after—Best Camper Award?

"Shall we, Max?"

"Good idea," Dad said. "These kids can earn their keep."

I rolled my eyes. "What about you earning yours? You didn't prepare sandwiches."

"Don't be fresh, Magenta. Anyway, I'm buying the coffee. Come along, Lianna."

"Your dad's a nice guy," Cal said, piling our plates into the dishpan. "It was really good of him to lend me his board like that. Well, it was really good of him to bring us here and organize this. Mom can't do this kind of thing."

I shrugged. "Dad and I go camping pretty often. It's not really a lot of trouble."

"Still," Cal said, "he hardly knows us. I mean, I thought he'd had all these e-mail conversations with Mom, but it turned out that was with you, so he really does hardly know us. Do you think he likes my mom?"

The question caught me off guard. "Do you mean like, or *like* like?" I asked.

"You know what I mean. Is he interested in her?"

"I honestly don't know. I haven't seen them holding hands or anything."

"I'd just like to get her settled," Cal said, handing me a wet plate. "Then I could focus more on my own stuff."

"You'd like to get her settled?" I dried the plate mechanically.

"Yes. Settled. I don't mean married or anything, just settled down. Calmer. Happier. With a life of her own. If she had someone like your dad, she'd be all right. I wouldn't have to worry about her."

"That's why I went online," I said. "For Dad. He seemed depressed. I'm not sure that I was right, though."

"He doesn't seem depressed," Cal said. "He seems too energetic to be depressed. Aren't depressed people supposed to sleep a lot and not want to go out? Or do you think meeting Mom has cheered him up?"

I didn't think Lianna had made the difference, but I couldn't tell Cal that, and I wasn't sure. Maybe she had. Maybe they'd get to the hand-holding stage by the end of the weekend. What did I know? I couldn't even write a kissing scene in the Chronicles.

"We should give them some alone time," I said. "So they can get to know each other."

Cal looked at me, his eyebrows raised. "Why exactly did you think I offered to clean up?" he asked. "Because I love washing dishes in cold soapy water?"

Mom had always told me that you could tell how a man was going to treat his girlfriends by the way he related to his mother. If that was true, Cal would be the perfect boyfriend. Unless he was going to be my stepbrother. That would really mess up the boyfriend bit. I didn't know what to hope for anymore.

"You do like Mom?" Cal asked. "I mean, I know she comes across as a little hopeless, but really, she isn't."

"Yes, I like her," I said. "But, anyway, it isn't me liking her that's important, is it? It's whether Dad likes her."

"And whether she likes Max," Cal pointed out.

Then there didn't seem to be much more to say about it, so we finished the dishes and played cards. I won five games out of seven. I liked Cal a lot, particularly when he told me Lady Luck rode on my shoulder. It was such a cool thing to think. I wondered if I could get Ricardo to say that to Rosa in the Chronicles. Would they play cards? They might even gamble. That would be a bit more action I could put in. What if he gambled for something really important?

"Penny for them?" Cal interrupted my thoughts.

"Just thinking of gambling," I said to him.

"Really? I don't think you should at your age."

"No, silly, this is for the Chronicles. I'm having problems with the action. As in, there isn't much. But if I had this character gamble for something really important—I don't know what—then it would be a bit more action and excitement."

"He could gamble for the hand of his lover," Cal said, without even stumbling over the word *lover*. "That would be pretty exciting. If he loses, she has to go off with the villain. If he wins, they live happily ever after. People still do that in fantasies."

"People still do that in real life. I mean, sometimes they must, don't you think?"

Cal shrugged. "Maybe the second time around, when they've learned how to do it better. Look, here they come. Do you think they like each other yet?"

We watched Spooky and Dad walking down the road to us. They weren't holding hands or even walking close.

"I don't think so," I said slowly. "They don't even look as though they're talking to each other."

"Darn it!" Cal said. "I really thought . . . oh, well, maybe it's still a little early."

I must admit, though, I felt a small shiver of pleasure at the thought that Dad and Spooky didn't really like each other. That way there was the remotest chance that Cal and I might be able to get to the *like*-like stage. If Lady Luck continued to ride on my shoulder.

# Confessions

"Well," Dad said as they arrived at the tent, "what a treat coming back from good coffee and a pleasant chat to discover the dishes already done. Thanks, kids. What is everyone planning for this afternoon? Lianna and I thought we might walk over to Squeaky Beach. What do you think?"

"That sounds great," I said.

"Except that Magenta and I thought we might hang out at the river," Cal cut in smoothly, beetling his eyebrows at me, "didn't we, Magenta?"

"That's right," I said quickly. "Some kids were going . . ."

"Fishing," Cal finished for me. "We thought we'd check out what they were catching."

"They had a canoe," I said, not to be outdone.

"Cal," Spooky said, "you can always go fishing, but you mightn't get another chance to go to Squeaky Beach for a long time. Please come."

"It's only sand that squeaks," I said.

"Cal!"

"I really want to see the fishing," Cal said. "I mean, we do. Magenta and me."

"And the canoe," I added, in case he'd forgotten.

"Cal, can I have a word in private?" Spooky said, and stepped forward to touch his arm.

"No, Mom." Cal stepped back, away from her. "It's just really simple. Magenta and I want to see the fishing and the canoe. You and Max can go to Squeaky Beach. You're not kids. You don't need supervision."

"Private?"

"There's no point, Mom."

"All right, then, I'll have to say this in front of everyone. I think it's lovely that you're trying to give Max and me some adult space, but Max and I are just friends, Cal. That's all."

"Yes, I know that, but you might—" Cal was blushing to the roots of his dark hair.

"No, we won't, Cal. Max has made it quite clear that he's interested in someone else."

"You're what? Who?" It was the first I'd ever heard of this.

"So you've just been leading Mom on?" Cal squared up to my Dad, and for a ridiculous moment I thought he was going to offer to fight him.

"I haven't led her on," Dad said. "I just offered to take you both camping, that's all."

"When you were interested in someone else? I call that a lousy way to treat someone."

"Cal," Spooky said, "adults can be friends, you know. That's what Max said the first time we met. It's not fair to accuse him of leading me on."

"You put yourself up on a dating site, and you're interested in someone else."

"He didn't put himself up," I said. "Still, Dad, you could have said something."

"I have," Dad said. "I told Lianna over coffee. I'd been trying to tell her through e-mail, but you know what that's like. It always came out wrong or something. So we've had our wires a bit crossed, but no harm's done, is it, Lianna?"

"Of course not, Max." Spooky smiled, but it was a sad kind of smile.

"I think it's despicable," Cal said angrily. "I think it's just despicable. Camping is . . . well, it's intimate. You share space with people. It hints at a bigger relationship than friendship."

"We have separate tents," I pointed out. "Dad, why didn't you tell me, not Spooky? You should have told me."

"Stop her calling her Spooky!" Cal shouted.

"Sorry. Dad, why didn't you say anything?"

"I wasn't sure if it was going anywhere. It didn't look as though it was."

"That's when you invited us camping," Cal said, "as a backup."

"That's not really what happened," Dad said, but he was looking at his shoes.

"You don't tell a girl you're interested in that you're just going camping with another girl, but it's okay because you're just friends," Cal said stubbornly. "I may only be a kid, but I do know that much."

"I think we should just stop all this," Spooky said, fanning herself with her hat. "It's not helping, Cal, darling. The point is that Max and I are just friends, and that's all that's going to happen, so why don't we walk to Squeaky Beach, the four of us together, and stop this bickering over nothing?"

"You aren't nothing," Cal said. "You're the most important person in my life, Mom. That's not nothing. I want you to be happy."

"Cal, darling, that's so wonderful of you. You're the most important person in my life, too, and always will be." I thought Spooky was going to cry, but she just sniffed and smiled a watery smile at us all. "I'm actually quite happy, Cal. I only went on the Internet dating site because you pestered me to. Of course it's lovely meeting new people, and I like both Max and Magenta. There wasn't that chemistry, though. Was there, Max?"

He looked a little embarrassed and cleared his throat but didn't actually say anything. It didn't matter, though, because Spooky was going to say it for them both.

"You know, darling, when you meet someone you really, really like, you do know right away. There's this little *frisson* of . . . well . . . *frisson*." Spooky said the word with a French accent that made it sound very exotic. "I had it with your father. I can remember so clearly."

"It didn't get you very far, then, did it, this chemical reaction?" Cal muttered.

"On the contrary," Spooky said, "it gave us fifteen wonderful years together. That's a long way, Cal. These days. It also gave us you."

"I want to know who she is," I said. If Spooky and Cal could stick to their argument, I could stick to mine. "Who is she, Dad? Have I met her?"

"Oh, yes, quite a lot," Dad said. "You know her."

"Who?"

"Sandra, the librarian."

"Not the grumpy one?" I couldn't remember which one Sandra was. I never looked at their name tags, ever.

"No, not the grumpy one. The smiley one with beautiful eyes."

"As if that tells me anything." I complained, but actually I thought I did know the one he meant. She'd let me off a couple of overdue fines.

"It's all very well to talk about chemistry," Cal said, "but when are you going to meet someone special, Mom? If Max can do it—no offense, Max—you must be able to."

"I'm sure there's someone out there," Spooky said. "It just isn't the right time yet. It is, however, the right time to head off to Squeaky Beach. Do let's go. I haven't been there since I was a teenager—about your age, Magenta. I remember loving it."

We walked to Squeaky Beach in two distinct pairs—Dad and me, Spooky and Cal. I didn't hear what they were talking about, because I was too busy asking Dad all sorts of questions about Sandra.

"So was Cal right, did you just have Spooky as a backup?" I couldn't believe that Dad would suddenly have two women interested in him. I shot a sideways glance at him. He looked okay dressed when you couldn't see his little pot belly because his shirt hung over it. "You'd better not ask Sandra camping," I told him, "because then she'll see you in a wet suit."

"What's wrong with that?"

"You've got this little pot," I said, patting it. Sometimes I rubbed it for luck, the way you're supposed to rub a statue of the Buddha.

"It's okay," Dad said, sucking in his tummy. "Not as bad as some."

"That's true. Does she know you're going bald?"

"It's pretty obvious, isn't it? To answer an earlier question, Magenta, which seems to me more important than these superficial ones, I suppose there might be a tiny little bit of truth in what Cal said. I'd invited Sandra out a couple of times, but she was always busy. I wasn't thinking of Lianna as more than a friend, but I did think that I should start living some kind of life, rather than hanging around hoping that Sandra was interested in me." Dad checked out where Spooky and Cal were and lowered his voice a little, so I had to lean in to hear what he was saying. It was crazy, because the wind was whipping around and the ocean was roaring off the rocks.

"I was also felt a little sorry for Lianna, and I thought, well, we could teach them to go camping and then she might feel a little less hopeless. She doesn't seem to have particularly high self-esteem. I kind of liked that, I suppose. Your mother was always confident and competent. I guess it made me feel a bit protective or something. Then, after I'd asked them, Sandra told me at the library that she was free this weekend. She'd been trying for ages to convince her mother to move into a nursing home, and her mother had finally found somewhere she thought would be all right."

"That's why you said it was bad timing." I remembered. "So are you going out with Sandra?"

"Yes," Dad said, and he couldn't hide his grin. "Yes, we're going out next weekend."

"I'll be at Mom's!"

"That's right. You'll be at your mother's." Dad didn't sound at all remorseful.

"So I won't get to meet her or anything."

"You've met her already," Dad said. "Anyway, I hope there'll be lots more chances."

Squeaky Beach seemed to cheer Spooky up. Actually, it was strange. Now that it was clear that she and Dad would only be friends, she seemed more relaxed and more natural. It was as if she was able to be herself. She stomped up the beach, making the sand squeak with every step. She grabbed Cal's arm, and they did it together. Then they did a fake tango, right there in the sand. It didn't matter that the entire beach watched. Spooky was nearly falling over, she was laughing so much.

"It's just how I remember!" she said. "Isn't it wonderful?"

"It's pretty good," I said carefully, "but it is just sand that squeaks."

"No, darling, that's where you're wrong. This beach was the thirteenth summer of my life," Spooky said, throwing out her hands. "It was my life that summer."

"A good summer, then?" Dad asked.

"A perfect summer," Spooky said. "A perfect summer, a perfect boy. I don't think he even knew I existed, but I wrote love poems to him the entire time. He was divine."

"Mom!"

Spooky shrugged at Cal and grinned. "Just divine."

I looked at Cal. Was he divine? No. I wouldn't have said that. Pretty good, but not divine. I wasn't even perfectly sure that Richard was divine when I thought about it. What was that *frisson*? My heart sometimes leaped against my rib cage when I saw Richard. Was that a *frisson*? It had done it with Cal, too, though—when we accidentally touched hands as he dealt out the cards. Could you have *frissons* with two boys?

We went swimming at Squeaky Beach, and even Spooky tucked her skirt up and waded in to her knees.

"I don't like swimming in the ocean," she told me. "I find it a bit confronting. You never know what might be lurking underneath. I'm afraid I don't give Cal all the opportunities he deserves as a boy. That's why I thought this trip with Max was so important. I was prepared to make an effort, even without the chemistry. For Cal's sake."

"You mean you would have gone out with Dad so Cal could go camping?"

"Sort of," Spooky said. "Perhaps not quite as bluntly as that sounds."

I shook my head. It seemed to me a good thing that Sandra had sorted all this out before it had gotten really messy. Otherwise Dad might have gone out with Spooky because he felt both that he should have a life (Hello! What had I been telling him?) and sorry for Spooky, and she would have gone out with Dad because she felt Cal should have a different life. This wasn't getting things right the second time around, as far as I could see.

"This *frisson* thing," I said to her, "can you have it with more than one boy?"

"At certain times in your life, of course," Spooky said. "Gosh, when I was in my teens! Even older. I guess the thing is that at a certain age, you don't act on it when it could hurt other people."

"So it's normal to have it for more than one boy?" I dragged her back to the topic. I wasn't going to hurt anyone.

"Perfectly normal, darling. Are they two boys from school?"

"No. No, not all."

Spooky looked at me. "Do they like you back?" she asked.

"I don't know," I said. "I don't think so. Not *like* like."

"Oh, well"–she touched my shoulder gently–"you've got years and years ahead of you. There are more things to life than just love, too. Don't forget that, Magenta."

"I won't. I'm going to be a famous fantasy writer. I'm in the middle of the first book of my first trilogy. I was just wondering. My mother doesn't talk about *frissons* or chemistry. They've got it, of course, Trib and Mom–they spend enough time smooching–but she's a teacher."

Spooky nodded. "Teachers have to be practical. It makes it harder."

By the time we got back to the campsite, it was getting dark. A strange, snorting kind of noise was coming from

Spooky's tent. She grabbed my arm, but only because I was closest.

"There's someone in my tent," she whispered. "Look!"

Sure enough, we could see something bulging out at the side.

"He's very short," I said.

"Or bent over?"

"Lianna"—Dad came up behind us, making us jump—"you haven't left food in the tent, have you?"

"Food? Anything open is in the cooler."

"Secured?"

"Of course."

"Nothing else?"

"I don't think so. Why?"

"That's not a person in your tent. It's a wombat."

"A wombat? Oh, my heavens. My face scrub. I bet it's after my face scrub."

"It's more likely to be after food."

"The stollen! I made a stollen. You can't put that in a cooler. It'd go soggy. It was in my pack. With my face scrub. What'll I do?"

Dad dealt with the wombat. He chased it out of the tent by banging the side it was bulging out of and yelling loudly. The wombat shot through the tent entrance. They can move really fast for such short, fat little things.

Spooky went in and came out with shreds of aluminum foil in her hands. "The stollen," she said. "All gone. Nothing left. All that work. At least my face scrub's intact. It has ground almonds in it, and honey. Just like the stollen, really."

"Never mind," Dad said, and he actually put his arm a little around her shoulders. "Think of it this way, that wombat's had the kind of artery-hardening treat wombats almost never get."

"You're right; there's quite a lot of butter in a stollen. I suppose we are better off without it. It does seem a shame, though. Don't look so downcast, Cal—you know I always make two. The other one's at home."

"What is stollen?" I asked.

"This fabulous cake Mom makes. She makes it for the café, too. It's really good. Marzipan and stuff."

"It's really a Christmas thing," Spooky said.

"It will make that wombat's Christmas for the next twenty years. Speaking of food"—Dad rubbed his belly—"do you need some help with dinner?"

"What a good idea. You said there were barbecues?"

We all trooped down to the closest barbecue, Cal and me carrying plates and mugs, while Dad took the cooler and Spooky carried two chairs.

"So what kind of sausages did you get?" I asked Spooky. I couldn't wait to find out. I knew they'd be some exotic thing that Dad would never buy in a million years.

"Sausages?"

"For dinner. Here, this one's free."

Spooky looked at the barbecue, and her face scrunched up. "We can't use this," she said. "It's filthy. It's greasy. Someone's been cooking sausages here. Or chops or something."

"That's what we're going to do," I said, "so it's fine. We're camping, Spoo . . . Lianna. That's what camping's about."

Spooky looked at me. "I'm not cooking on sausage fat," she said. "Cal and I are vegetarians."

"Vegetarians!" Dad and I said together.

"You had chicken at our place," I said.

"I tried not to," Spooky said. "I ate mostly salad. Although white meat isn't so bad."

"We always have sausages," I said. "We're camping."

"We never have sausages," Spooky said, "and since I've brought the food, we're having tofu."

"Tofu?" Dad said as though it was a rude word.

"That's right. Marinated tofu."

"It's delicious," Cal said, "but Mom's right: we'll have to clean up this sausage fat first."

"With what, exactly?" I asked. We weren't equipped to clean barbecues.

Spooky looked at my dad expectantly. "You seem to be the sausage expert," she pointed out quietly but firmly.

So Dad and I labored away, cleaning the barbecue with paper towels, a spatula, and some detergent.

"We always have sausages," I hissed at him. "Why didn't you bring the food?"

"She offered, Magenta. Don't get so worked up. I'm sure tofu's fine. You can have sausages tomorrow night."

"I'm at Mom's tomorrow night. She never has sausages. Full of preservatives. We're going to starve."

"Don't be so silly, Magenta. We won't starve."

"Tofu is *healthy*." I'd been so looking forward to sausages.

"Magenta!"

"Okay, okay."

Finally the barbecue passed Spooky's inspection, and she was ready to cook. She talked about everything before she cooked it.

"This tofu, which is organic, has been marinated in satay sauce, perfect for barbecuing. With that we'll just fry up some mushrooms and peppers. If you could just brush the tops of these mushrooms, please, Max. No need to peel them, just dust the top with a paper towel. That's right."

It wasn't sausages, but it was pretty good. There was a salad with crunchy noodles in it that almost made up for it. I had two helpings of the satay tofu, but Dad had three. Spooky smiled triumphantly.

"Pity there's no dessert," Cal said wistfully. "I used to think wombats were cute."

We did have hot chocolates, though, with marshmallows in them. I wondered if Sandra the librarian would be as well prepared.

# How to Kiss, the Perfect Skirt, and an Outline

Of course Mom wanted to know all about the camping "date." She laughed when I told her about the tofu and the wombat but didn't laugh when I told her about Sandra. Instead she said, "A librarian, eh?" and sighed a bit.

"You don't mind?" I asked. "You can't, Mom. You and Trib are getting married!"

"No. Why should I? I don't mind at all. I'd like your dad to be happy. Still, I didn't expect him to be interested in a librarian. That's practically like an English teacher."

"Not really; librarians don't teach. It's quite different. There's a lot of technology involved. That's probably what they've got common."

"I doubt it," Mom said. "Hasn't he given up technology?"

"Well, yes. It could still be what they have in common. Couldn't it?"

"I don't know, and it's not actually any of my business. You're right. I guess I'm just curious who has caught his eye after all these years. I can't explain it, Magenta."

I patted her arm. "It's okay. I'm curious, too."

"You've seen her, though. Is she—you know—pretty?"

"If she's the one I think she is, yes, she's kind of pretty. In a middle-aged kind of way."

There was a pause, and Mom turned away to stir the soup. She looked into the saucepan in an interested way and asked, "Slim? Or plump?"

"Mom!"

"Come on, Magenta. You can tell me."

"I don't even know if she's the right one."

"Plumper than me?"

"I don't know."

"That means she isn't. I'm thinking of getting myself a gym membership for a personal pre-wedding present."

"Mom, you look fine."

"Still, for the wedding. You were the one who suggested a diet, Magenta."

"Only because you went on and on about the plump roses. Have you found a skirt yet?"

"No," Mom said, "but I feel closer. I've found several nearly-there prospects. I thought we might go and have a look this weekend?"

"Yeah, sure." I tried to sound enthusiastic.

"It won't take too long," Mom said. "I've narrowed down the field. Then I thought we could go to a bookshop. Just for a change of pace. There must be a book you need. We'll go to the one with the coffee shop and those great little party cakes."

Clearly her pre-wedding diet wasn't a priority at this stage. "Okay, that sounds great." Mom in a bookshop was always good news. She had this idea that spending money on books wasn't like spending real money. It was more of an investment in the future. I loved going book shopping with Mom.

"Speaking of books, how are the Chronicles coming along?"

"Slowly," I said, "but steadily. I'd hoped to finish the first volume this year, but I'm not sure that I'm going to get there. I can't write about kissing."

"Why?"

"Mom! Because I haven't done it yet. Anyway, it's kind of embarrassing. What can you say about kissing?"

"They kissed. What more do you want?" Mom said. "I mean, it's fantasy you're writing, not romance."

"'They kissed' is a little abrupt, isn't it?"

"It depends on the context, doesn't it? He drew her gently into his arms and looked down at her heart-shaped face. She was the most beautiful creature he had ever seen. They kissed. That doesn't sound abrupt, does it?"

I was impressed. "Did you just think that up?"

"Well, it's hardly Shakespeare," Mom said, "but you probably don't want the whole kissing thing to interrupt the main drama, do you?"

The main drama? "The main drama keeps changing," I said. "I can't seem to make up my mind what happens."

"You could try doing a chapter outline," Mom said, "like a kind of timetable? Just jot down your ideas for each chapter. Would that help?"

"Like an essay outline?" This was beginning to sound like homework. That was one of the traps of having a teacher for a mother. Good things could quickly change into education, which was sometimes interesting, like sushi and Tokyo street fashion, and sometimes really boring, like pop music and the role of feminism. This outline stuff sounded as if it could quickly turn badly educational.

"No, nothing like an essay outline," Mom said, slicing bread. "Honestly, Magenta—you're trying to be a writer, not a grade-A student. It's a different thing entirely."

The benefits of being an English teacher's daughter include access to an unlimited supply of glitter pens and huge pieces of construction paper. By bedtime I had a chapter outline written up on a big piece of paper I could pin to my wall.

The trouble was, as Trib pointed out when he poked his head in to say good night, that a good half of the chapter squares were empty.

"It's a work in progress," I told him.

"'Progress' might be pushing it," he said.

"At least you know what's missing now," Mom said, giving Trib the kind of look she gave her students who'd overstepped some line.

I stuck my tongue out at Trib, but I knew what he meant. The blank squares stared at me like blind eyes.

"I don't want to put you off," Trib said. "I'm in awe of what you have done, Magenta. I can't write a lousy five-page report without tearing out my hair. Don't get me wrong. You're amazing."

"Thanks, Trib."

"It does make you realize how much work goes into

these books, doesn't it?" he continued. "I mean, at the very least you'll come out the other end with a deeper understanding of the whole process. That's got to be something."

"I'll have a trilogy when I come out the other end," I said haughtily. "This is my life, Trib. This is who I am." I waved at the outline tacked on the wall. I sounded a great deal more confident than I felt. There were a lot of blank squares, and this was only the first book.

"I'm sure it will all come to you," Mom said briskly. "The more life experience you have, the easier you'll find it."

"I don't really need life experience," I said. "I need more plot, that's what I need. It's a fantasy, after all. I need drama and plot."

"Life experience will give that to you in spades," Trib said, laughing. "Just go clothes shopping with your mom!"

I liked the way Trib said "your mom" as though she was really special. He rested his hand on her shoulder then, and when she smiled at him, I knew she'd been telling the truth about just being curious about Sandra and Spooky. Even though I hadn't wanted Dad and Mom to ever split up, I knew she was happy with Trib. When they were like this, it seemed that their happiness spilled over onto everything, including me. They made me feel safe and cozy.

"I'm shopping with her tomorrow," I said. "But we're going to a bookshop afterward."

"Glad it's your schedule, not mine," Trib said. "I keep telling her she'll look great in anything. Honestly, Tammy, you could wear a potato sack and I'd still say I do and mean it with all my heart."

"Trib, that's lovely of you, darling. I know the whole clothes thing is superficial, but I still do want the nearly perfect outfit. I've given up on perfect. Nearly perfect will do."

"It's a girl-thing," I said sleepily. "We should get Polly to cast the nearly perfect spell."

We didn't need Polly, though. After two hours and eighteen minutes of searching, we arrived at a little shop that looked hopeless on the outside because the window was filled with old ladies' clothes. We hesitated at the threshold, and a shop lady came and practically pounced on us, dragging us inside.

She asked Mom what she was looking for in this very bossy tone. Mom's mouth tightened a little bit, but she doesn't like being rude, so she explained.

The woman looked her up and down as though measuring her. "A garden party?" she repeated.

"I think so. Yes, probably. Depending on the weather. And the skirt, of course."

"I have just the thing," the woman said. "It will be perfect."

It was. It was a burgundy lace skirt that flounced at the sides. There were paler, pinker bits around the hem. Underneath the lace was a mesh skirt in the same burgundy, and the mesh part hung down lower in some places than the lace. It wasn't just nearly perfect. It was utterly perfect. Within five minutes the shop lady had bustled Mom into a silky shirt that went with it and screamed garden party. Or rather, whispered it seductively.

"It's heavenly," Mom said. "I don't care how much it is. I'm just going to hand over my credit card and close my eyes."

She had to open them to sign the bill, though, and she was so pleasantly surprised that she bought me three books, not just one, and we had chai tea and three party cakes between the two of us, because it was really wedding research, rather than actual eating.

# The Tough Guide and Socks

The first thing I did when I got back to Dad's was to look around for evidence of his date with Sandra. It wasn't hard to find. There on my bed was a book, *The Tough Guide to Fantasyland* by Diana Wynne Jones.

"Sandra thought you might be interested in that." Dad had followed me. "She said that although Diana Wynne Jones writes fantasy, she has a cynical attitude to some of the problems with the genre. She said she hopes it won't put you off and, if you feel it might, to stop reading it immediately."

"That's a lot of instructions to come with a book," I said.

Dad shrugged. "I'm just passing on the message."

I looked at him. He looked less slouchy somehow, better put together than he normally did. It wasn't just that he was wearing my favorite red-brown shirt, but also he'd had a haircut, so there was less gray showing around his ears. More than all that, though, he looked happy.

"So it went well?"

"It did. There was a moment of awkwardness," Dad said, "because after the movie Sandra wanted coffee at Lianna's friend's. That could have been tricky."

"So what happened?"

"I didn't know what to say," Dad admitted. "I could hardly tell Sandra the whole story at that point."

"Dad! You didn't lie on your first date?"

"No, of course not, Magenta. We went into the café. Sandra said they had the best selection of herb teas, so I could hardly say no. Lianna was working in the kitchen, but she came out when she saw us. It was very civilized, Magenta. It was . . . what would you say? Cool. It was cool."

"Did you see Cal?"

"No, of course not. It was past his bedtime, but Lianna did say he'd wanted to send you an e-mail but didn't have your e-mail address. She didn't know his, either, but she did give me Cal's cell phone number. I said you'd send him a text."

"Great!" It might not mean anything. Was he just being polite? Or did he really want to hear from me? A text wasn't as bad as having to make a phone call, though. I could probably manage a little text.

"You kids got along well, didn't you?"

"He was okay," I said. "I liked him. You know, for a boy."

"Boys are just people."

"No, Dad, boys aren't people. They're like a separate species. So he was pretty good for an alien."

I didn't hear much more about Dad's date. He just

repeated that it had gone well and yes, he expected to see more of Sandra in the future. She had a son, too, but he was younger than Cal, younger than me. His name was Toby.

"That's a dog's name," I said. "Not a boy's name."

"Don't say that in front of Sandra! Or Toby, for that matter."

"Have you met him?"

"No, of course not. It's in the early days yet, Magenta. Neither of us wants to rush things."

"Mom found the perfect skirt," I said without thinking.

"Perfect for what?"

"For, you know, getting married in?"

"Oh. That's good."

I thought I'd put my foot in my mouth, but when I looked at Dad, he was still smiling in the same odd, dreamy way he had been since I'd arrived home.

I called Polly and passed on the Sandra-news. Annoyingly, she took credit.

"It couldn't have been your spell," I said. "How could a love spell you made for Dad and Lianna work for Dad and Sandra?"

"I didn't want to tell you at the time of the camping trip," Polly said, "but when I made it, my hand was resting on an old library book."

"So?"

"It's clear, isn't it? Library book equals librarian equals Sandra. Do you think she'd let me off my overdue fine if I told her it was my spell that made her fall in love? I seem to have had this book out for two and a half months."

"I doubt it," I said. Polly the witch was getting on my nerves. "I think she'd just double it, because you're clearly out of your mind."

"Thanks a lot," Polly said, but she sounded less offended than I'd hoped. Then Dad called me to dinner, so I was saved from any more of her spell disasters.

It wasn't until after dinner that Dad said casually, "I may have a job prospect, too."

I gaped at Dad, putting my piece of pizza down. "A job?"

"The first steps to one," Dad said. "I'm going to do some IT consulting for the Greens—the Green party, that is. It won't be well paid, but it will get me a foot in the door. It's something I've been working on for a while. Connecting sustainability with decent technology. It's important for our future, Magenta. I want to live the life, not just talk the talk."

"So you'd be working for the Greens?"

Dad nodded. His smile stretched right across his face, and his eyes were all lit up from behind as though they had candles burning in them.

"Dad, that's fantastic! That's so cool."

"It is, isn't it? It's what I've been wanting for a long time now. It won't make us wealthy, Magenta, but I'll be able to help your Mom out with some child support, and there'll be a bit more money around."

"I think it's just great that you've got a job!" I said. "That's what matters, Dad."

"It took a while," Dad said. "I was worried, I tell you. It was hard to keep the faith for a while there."

"I'm really proud of you." I got up and went around to his side of the table and gave him a kiss and a big hug. "Really proud."

"Thanks, baby. I'm proud of you, too."

"I haven't done anything."

"You tried to do something," Dad said, raising his glass of water. "To us. To Magenta, matchmaker and fantasy writer, and to Max, optimistic IT consultant."

"Failed matchmaker," I said. "Was Lianna okay?"

"She seemed fine," Dad said. "She made us eat a piece of stollen. She told Sandra about the wombat. She and Sandra got on fine. Did you know a guy owns that café?"

"So?"

"Just that I'd always assumed a woman did, from how Lianna talked."

"What was the stollen like?"

"Really good, of course. Lianna is an excellent cook."

"Is Sandra?"

"I don't know," Dad admitted, "but that's not really important, is it?"

Sandra may or may not have been able to cook, but she certainly knew her books. Which you'd expect from a librarian. I browsed through the Diana Wynne Jones before dinner. I could see why the book came with that long message. It was weird. She had the kind of mind that reminded me of Polly. Like, for example, who would have thought to notice that no one in fantasy books wears socks? Come to think of it, socks aren't exactly a highlight of most other books I've read. Some of the stuff she talked about was pretty funny, like how crystal balls play a soundless video of your future. I wasn't sure how it was going to help me write the Chronicles, although I was determined now to mention someone's socks. That way if Diana Wynne Jones ever updated her guide, she'd have to say, "except in *The Chronicles of Forrdike Castle.*"

After dinner, Dad told me to put my running shoes on.

"What?"

"New routine," he said. "An after-dinner run."

"A run?"

"Yep. You wanted to train for track, didn't you?"

"That was ages ago. I don't need to train again until next year."

"If you start now," Dad said, lacing up a pair of new sneakers, "you'll be at least eight months fitter than you would be if you only begin next year."

"I'm not sure that I want to be eight months fitter."

"Well, I do. You can be my motivational trainer. That will entail jogging alongside your poor old dad and shouting words of encouragement. Come on, Magenta; you wanted me to get out more."

"Yeah, but I didn't want you to run out. Just walk—preferably to the movies or dinner. Not an evening jog. You might have a stroke."

"Then it's twice as important that you're with me. You've got the cell."

I knew he was joking, but there was still a certain amount of logic to his argument. I wasn't sure that Dad, who hadn't run a mile in living memory, should be allowed out jogging by himself.

"I guess I should do something," I said, grabbing my running shoes. "After all, writing is all sitting down. Unless you're getting life experience. Which clearly I can't get while I'm still at school. I'll come with you, but can we go down backstreets, where we're not likely to bump into anyone we know?"

"Sure," Dad said, "and not a huge distance our first time out. This will be fun, Magenta. We've been missing a bit of fun, haven't we?"

"You may have," I told him, "but I've been fine. Really."

I met Sandra the next day at the library. I'd taken my chapter outline up to photocopy so that I could have one copy at Mom's and one at Dad's. I thanked her for the book, of course, and told her about the socks.

"But really," I said, "you wouldn't mention socks in a normal book, would you? Not unless they were special socks someone had given you or really cool knee-high ones. We just take socks for granted."

"That's true," she said, "but maybe Diana Wynne Jones is being a bit sarcastic."

"I'm going to mention socks in the Chronicles," I told her. "I'm going to make sure I mention them a fair amount, really. I've already thought of one place where it would be natural to think of socks, and that's with my witch, Holly, down in the dungeon. She could be regretting not wearing socks, because it would be cold down there."

"I think that's a great idea," Sandra said, "but maybe you don't want to talk about them too much. It might be a little odd."

"Just when it's relevant," I said.

We talked for a little while about books while she was helping me with the photocopier. She smiled at Dad quite a lot, but they didn't kiss or anything. I suppose you can't kiss at work. I didn't hear them call each other darling or anything like that, either, even though I was listening hard all the time. I must have missed something, though, because when we got home, Dad said that Sandra was coming around after the library closed and they were going for a walk.

I stayed at home. I didn't want to cramp Dad's romantic style. But also I wanted to get on with my sock idea and the Chronicles. I also wanted to see if Mom was right and I could get Ricardo and Lady Rosa to kiss, just like that. Plus I needed to text Cal, and I couldn't do that with anyone else around.

I did the socks first. The Chronicles were familiar. Texting Cal wasn't.

> *Holly must have drifted off to sleep despite the rat scuffles. When she woke up, her feet were cold. She should have worn socks, she thought, rather than her best slip-on shoes. Thick, woolly socks would have made a considerable difference to her comfort at this point. She considered asking the guard if he could provide her with a pair the next time he came with food or water. Or perhaps she could give Lady Burgundy a little information in return for a pair? Her feet were really very, very cold.*

Hmm. Well, I could understand why most fantasy writers left socks out—they were hardly the most interesting thing to write about. But I'd done it, and I wasn't unhappy with the result.

Next I tried the kiss.

> *Ricardo bent his head over Lady Rosa's just as she was looking up at him.*
>
> *"The moon . . ." she said quickly, "it's very . . ."*
>
> *"As are you . . . beautiful," he said, and for the briefest of moments, their lips met in the lightest of kisses. Then there was a noise at the great doors, and they drew quickly apart.*

Kisses were certainly more interesting to write about than socks. How I got to that kiss was to imagine Cal kissing someone. Not me necessarily. Just some girl. I'd tried to do that with Richard, of course, but it just hadn't worked. Maybe because I'd always thought Richard's kisses would be more . . . intense? Which I just couldn't imagine, let alone write about.

This kiss was just right. I was very pleased with myself. Suddenly the blank squares in the chapter plan didn't look so bad. They weren't vacant so much as waiting to be filled.

It was a good thing I'd stayed at home, because just as I was sitting on my bed trying to work out a text message that was both casual and friendly, my cell phone rang.

It was Mom.

"Listen, baby," she said, "you know the wedding guest list?"

I didn't really, but I said yes anyway.

"Trib and I are going through it now. Naturally people can bring guests, and Richard—you know Richard?"

Of course I knew Richard. What a silly question.

"Well, he's bringing his new girlfriend."

"His what?" Richard had a girlfriend? Since when?

"Girlfriend," Mom said very clearly. "He's been going out with this girl for a couple of months."

A couple of months? How come I didn't know? I felt as though I might throw up.

"So I was wondering, sweetie, if there was someone you'd like to invite? You know, Polly or someone?"

Richard was going out with someone! He was probably kissing her, intensely. They'd dance together at the wedding, if there was going to be dancing. He'd take her out on the parapet and kiss her intensely. In front of me. It was almost too much to bear thinking about.

"What's she like?" I asked. "Have you met her? Is she . . . beautiful?"

"Only once," Mom said. "She seemed okay. Quite pretty. Now, back to you: who would you like to bring as a guest?"

I wondered about Cal. For a moment I thought of Cal and me walking hand in hand through the garden party. I thought of Cal leaning over to kiss me, a feather-kiss, the lightest of kisses. We'd dance next to Richard and his girlfriend, and I wouldn't even look at Richard.

"What's her name?"

"Umm, hold on a sec. I've written it down somewhere. Here it is. Here name's Serena. Wasn't that the name of some witch on a television program?"

"I don't know." I couldn't really invite Cal. I didn't know him that well. A wedding was an intimate thing—

more than camping. If your crush was with someone else at a wedding, you really needed someone totally on your side to be with you. You needed your best friend. "Can I bring Polly, then?"

"Of course, darling." Mom sounded very relieved. "I think that's a great idea. Better get back to it, then. Love you."

"Love you, too. Have a good time."

*Serena*, I thought when I hung up. Serena was one of those names that made me think of creepy things. I forgot about texting Cal. I had more important things to do, really. I wasn't at all sure that a boy would fit into my life at the moment. Not with the cross-country practice and my father to keep on track. Obviously his romance needed all the help it could get, considering they were just smiling at each other. Then there were the Chronicles.

> *Ricardo sat down on the bed to take off his socks. The bed was a magnificent four-poster, one with midnight-blue drapes. Serena would love this, he thought, dropping his socks in a pile of dirty washing. She loved luxury. It was a pity. . . . He wished he could stop thinking about her. He was here to woo Lady Rosa. She had beauty, intelligence, and money. Serena, however, was an enchantress who had long ago stolen his heart. He put his head in his hands. When would he see her again? When would she let him come back to her?*

Fantastic! Socks and added plot. The Chronicles were moving fast. I could fill in a few more squares, I thought.

At this rate I'd have the first book written by the time Trib and Mom got married. That would leave the second book to finish before Dad and Sandra got married. Which they were sure to do. Everyone loves to live happily ever after, even if it's only for a little while.

I'd make sure something ghastly happened to Serena—in the Chronicles, of course. In real life she'd probably turn out to be really lovely and lend me her special nail polish or something. That's what I love about writing—you can change real life around. In the Chronicles, Serena could break Ricardo's heart, and there Rosa Burgundy would be, waiting. Maybe not right away, of course. First of all she might rescue Holly and go to find her father. On the way they could get lost and be helped by a handsome young boy called Callum, the son of a gypsy woman. Maybe Mom was right and life experience helped even a fantasy writer like myself.

In the interests of life experience, I texted Cal. It was just a little message saying hi. Nothing even an alien boy could take amiss or read anything into. I'd hardly pushed Send when my cell phone rang.

"Hey," Cal's voice said, sounding a little wobbly, as though the connection wasn't particularly good.

"Oh, hi," I said.

"I have some credit on my phone," he said. "What's been happening?"

I told him about Diana Wynne Jones, the socks, and Sandra.

"I could be the first fantasy writer in the world to bring in socks," I said.

"Gee, maybe you should e-mail her and let her know."

"She doesn't have an e-mail address," I said. I'd already looked her up online. "She's really old, you know."

"Maybe you should write her a letter, you know, the old-fashioned way?"

That was such a good idea that, without thinking, I told Cal that if he ever wanted to come around for a few hundred games of sic bo, he was welcome.

"Hey, that'd be cool. Actually, I wanted to know if you'd like to come to the Fall Equinox Lantern Parade. You have to make a lantern. Well, you wouldn't have to, because we've got two, and Mom can't take hers, because she's serving cakes."

By the time he hung up, I had a kind of date. The lantern parade sounded like a good thing for a fantasy writer to get involved in. This life-experience stuff was beginning to work for me.

I sat down at my desk and wrote "Chapter Five" in big, curling letters.

Lady Rosa willed herself to stay awake until the merriment had ended. She wouldn't have slept, anyway. The kiss from Ricardo, rudely interrupted as it had been, burned on her lips. She kept touching her mouth and marveling at the thought of his lips on hers. It was a shame that she had to leave when they'd barely become acquainted, but her father and his whereabouts were more important than anything else.

In what she judged were the early hours of the morning, she stole down the long passageway to the dungeon.

"Who is it?" whispered a frightened little voice when she opened the great door to Holly's cell.

"Lady Rosa. There's nothing to be frightened of. I've come to get you out of here. We have to go and find my father."

"Oh. All right. That's a sensible idea, I suppose," Holly said, getting to her feet. "I'll be happy to assist in any way possible, but before we do anything, I really need a pair of socks."